DEFENCE AGAINST THE DARK ARTS

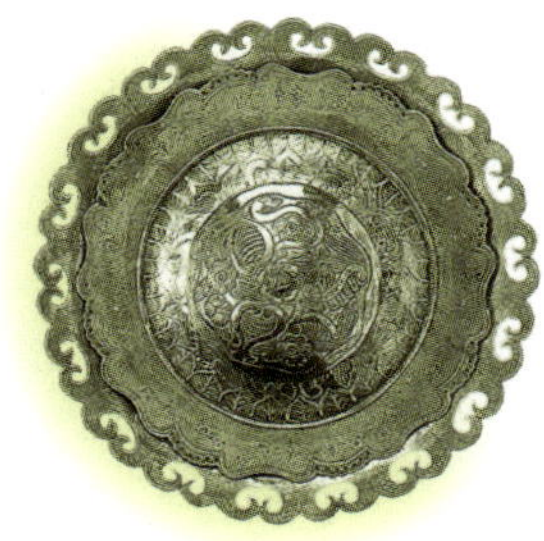

DEFENCE AGAINST THE DARK ARTS

FRANCIS MELVILLE

Eagle Editions

A QUANTUM BOOK

Published by Eagle Editions Ltd
11 Heathfield
Royston
Hertfordshire SG8 5BW

This edition printed 2008

This book is produced by
Quantum Books
6 Blundell Street
London
N7 9BH

ISBN 978-1-84573-376-6

QUMPSPR

Printed in China by
Midas Printing International Ltd

Contents

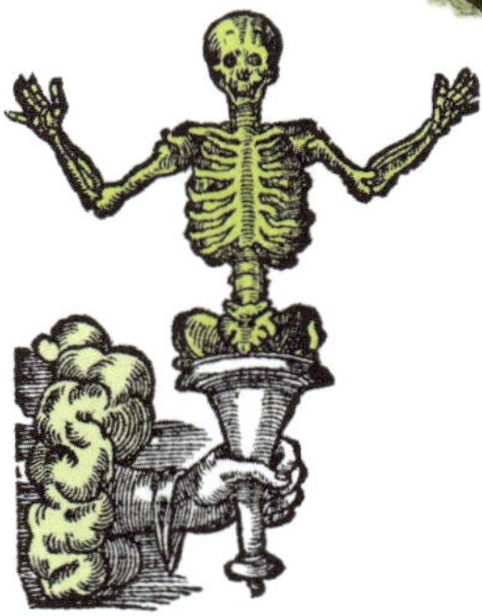

Introduction

The Dark Arts are still widely practiced throughout the world. Although they are divided into many forms, the techniques that are used have much in common. This book examines the principal magical techniques, the occult traditions from which they spring, and a variety of methods for building a magic shield of protection against them.

The Dark Arts Defined

The terms "DARK ARTS" and "BLACK ARTS" actually refer to all magic, *whether positive or negative.* The concept of magic is only dark in the sense that the forces it uses are occult, *which means* **hidden** *or* **invisible**. The terms "dark" and "black" originally referred to EGYPT, the birthplace of the Western magical tradition. Egypt was known as the "*Black Land,*" because of the **dark alluvial silt** that covers the fields during the NILE'S yearly floods. The Black Arts, therefore, meant "*the arts of the black land*" or "*the Egyptian arts,*" and included such harmless practices as ASTROLOGY. Nowadays, however, the Dark Arts have come to refer to **black magic** and **sorcery**, *and that is the sense in which the term is used in this book.*

Origins of Magic

Magic has a very ancient history; *indeed, it is as old as HUMANITY itself.* Our ancestors *PERCEIVED* the world in a way that we would understand as **fundamentally magical**, were we able to *SHARE* their *VISION*. For them, the whole of creation LIVED and SPARKLED with **intelligence** and **personality**. What we think of as the natural world—*the landscape, the plant and animal kingdoms, and the elements*—was for them ANIMATED by **sentient entities** and **spirits**. *The higher spirits of the* OCEANS, SKIES, *and* HEAVENLY BODIES *were worshipped as DEITIES.*

As they developed rituals and prayers to HONOR *the* SPIRITS, early humans learned how they could COMMUNICATE with them directly and MANIPULATE their lesser manifestations to act in accordance with their will. **Thus was magic born.**

An Eye for an Eye

While there has been a NEW AGE tendency to romanticize our prehistoric magical past as a **harmonious golden age,** this was clearly not always the case. The earliest known magical artefacts were **amulets** *designed to protect the wearer from evil.* There is also very early evidence of *RITUAL MUTILATION* among PALEOLITHIC tribes. *Similar customs that exist in parts of the world today indicate that such practices serve as a form of RECONCILIATION with occult forces.* Ancient myths and legends teem with **demons** and **dangerous deities**. *These were the forces with which our ancestors had to contend.* In developing methods to protect themselves, however, they also learned how to *MANIPULATE EVIL* for their own ends. **Thus was black magic born.**

Persecution

As humans developed their TECHNICAL ABILITIES and assumed *GREATER CONTROL* over their *MATERIAL ENVIRONMENT, their perceptions became increasingly limited to the material domain.* In EUROPE and the great empires of ASIA, **religion** became more **abstract**. PRIESTHOODS *existed alongside* MONARCHIES, *and state religion exercised its own powerful magic.* At the same time, simple INTERACTIONS with nature spirits were considered a **pagan vice**, and were increasingly REPRESSED by religious authorities. Religious **intolerance**, coupled with a genuine **horror** of sorcery and malevolent witchcraft, *led to the persecution of all forms of magic.*

Revival

The MAGICAL WORLD **shrank** as a result of **dogmatic** *RELIGIONISTS* and *RATIONALISTS* alike, *and it was not until the late 19th century that the occult revival began in Europe and North America,* culminating in the NEW AGE movement that has blossomed in the last 40 years. Phenomena such as *ANGELS, NATURE SPIRITS, DIVINATION, SPIRITUAL HEALING,* and *ALCHEMY* are of growing interest to ACADEMICS, SCIENTISTS, and the GENERAL PUBLIC alike, while magic is now being more **widely practiced** in the West than at any time in the last 400 years.

Abuses

Black magic utilizes **destructive forces** to cause **harm**, *while white magic employs* **harmonious forces** *to serve the* **light**. Magic is colored by the intent of the practitioner. Human nature being what it is, most magic therefore tends to be "*gray.*" Although many people employ magic for ETHICAL PURPOSES, there are others whose motives are **selfish** and **malevolent**. *Those who practice the occult sciences for selfish ends can be* **dangerous enemies**.

Self-protection

The majority of suspected "*hexings*" (curses) and **magical attacks** prove to be DELUSORY, *the product of fear*, OUR GREATEST ENEMY. In genuine cases, however, it pays to be prepared. **Never be tempted to retaliate in kind**—this would simply be delving into the Dark Arts yourself, leading you *FARTHER* from the *LIGHT* and deeper into a state of FEAR and PAIN. The greatest defense is *SELF-KNOWLEDGE, which can be enhanced by developing a DEEPER UNDERSTANDING of the forces at play in the UNIVERSE.*

PART ONE of this book explains the basic principles of all the main forms of magic and their abuses, while PART TWO shows how you can protect yourself from negative influences, whether deliberate or unconscious.

Part One

The Dark Ar

The Dark Arts have many NEGATIVE associations but the term actually refers to all the techniques of ORGANIZED MAGIC, whether GOOD or EVIL. Magic is sa to be dark because the forces it uses are occult— HIDDEN INVISIBLE —and not necessarily evil. However, the tern Dark Arts is generally used to refer to the use of OCCULT techniques for SELFISH ENDS.

Chapter 1
Satanism

Satanism is an **inversion** of CHRISTIANITY. It is a **revolt** against Christian SOCIAL and MORAL CODES that *REJECTS* Christian values and *WORSHIPS* Satan—*the Christian devil*—as the ANTICHRIST and *TRUE KING* of the **material world**. Satanists **repudiate** Christ and **scorn** virtues such as *HUMILITY* and *UNCONDITIONAL LOVE*, GLORIFYING instead in **pride**, **individualism**, and **hedonism**.

The Antichrist

"Satan is that angel who was PROUD enough to believe himself God; BRAVE enough to buy his independence at the price of eternal suffering and torture; BEAUTIFUL enough to have adored himself in full divine light; STRONG enough to still reign in darkness amidst agony, and to have made himself a throne out of this INEXTINGUISHABLE PYRE."

ELIPHAS LÉVI, *History of Magic*

Unlike the *PAGAN RELIGIONS* that Christianity replaced, *Satanism is not so much non-Christian as* **anti-Christian**. In fact, SATANISM is a **product** of CHRISTIANITY. The idea of a *CULT* of *SATAN* first appeared in *EUROPE* in the late 15th century when a PAPAL BULL redefined witchcraft, *hitherto considered as a* **relic** *of paganism*, as *SATANISM*. This new definition provided the HOLY OFFICE of the INQUISITION with a new target on which to **concentrate** its energies. *Apart from CONFESSIONS extracted under* **torture**, there is no **evidence** that a satanic *CULT* of *WITCHES*, *as defined by the church*, ever existed except in the *FEVERED IMAGINATION* of the INQUISITORS.

Christian Paranoia

PERIODIC BOUTS of Christian paranoia, however, have ensured that a **modus operandi** of correct *SATANIC BEHAVIOR* is repeatedly presented to those who would like to **indulge** in some particularly *OUTRAGEOUS BEHAVIOR*. The PRINCE of DARKNESS owes his **identity** not to his FOLLOWERS, but to his ENEMIES, *for SATANISM could not exist without the* **writings** *of CHRISTIAN ANTI-SATANISTS*. Most satanic groups are **ephemeral** and made up of YOUNG PEOPLE with very little *OCCULT KNOWLEDGE*. As they often seek little more than an OUTLET for **youthful rebellion**, *they represent little threat to society.*

The Black Mass

The **principal rite** of Satanism is the **Black Mass**, *which is a DIABOLICAL INVERSION of the Christian Mass.* In the *CHRISTIAN EUCHARIST*, the priest magically **transmutes** the *BREAD* or *COMMUNION WAFER* and *WINE* into the **body** and **blood** of Christ through the process known as TRANSUBSTANTIATION. *Satanists believe that by* **subverting** *this magical process*, they can partake of the *ESSENCE* of the ANTICHRIST and share his *INFERNAL POWERS.*

Early History

The order of *WARRIOR MONKS* known as the KNIGHTS TEMPLAR were accused of **subverting** the Holy Mass for *EVIL ENDS* in the early 14th century, *as was the 15th-century French nobleman* GILLES DE RAIS. Although several others were also **accused** of holding BLACK MASSES during the next two centuries, *it is not until the end of the 17th century that we find* **concrete evidence** *of the performance of* **Black Masses**.

In *PARIS* in **1679** a fashionable FORTUNE-TELLER named LA VOISIN was **arrested** along with more than 300 followers and ACCUSED of *POISONING* and *SACRILEGE.* She was said to have obtained **babies** for **ritual sacrifice** during Black Masses conducted by a *RENEGADE PRIEST* called the ABBÉ GUIBOURG. It was claimed that these masses were

CONDUCTED over the **naked body** of a woman and that at the moment of CONSECRATION of the host, *the baby's throat was cut.* The BLOOD was collected in a **chalice** and OFFERED UP in prayer to the **demons** ASTAROTH and ASMODEUS. At LA VOISIN'S **trial**, it was revealed that many of these Black Masses were held *at the request of one of* LOUIS XIV's *mistresses,* the MARQUISE DE MONTESPAN, who was determined to retain her ROYAL LOVER'S affections. *While the* MARQUISE *and the other* NOBLES *implicated escaped* PUNISHMENT, 36 commoners were **executed** and LA VOISIN was *BURNED ALIVE* as a **witch**.

Book of the Black Mass

Two centuries later PARIS again provided would-be *SATANISTS* with information on how to **conduct** themselves, this time in the form of the **novel** *Là-Bas* by J.K. HUYSMANS. *In the novel* HUYSMANS *explored the themes of Satanism,* describing *BLACK MAGIC* rituals, including the **Black Mass**, in which the **Catholic service** was recited BACKWARD, the **crucifix** INVERTED, the **host** DEFILED, and the **rite** followed by a *SEXUAL ORGY.* A Black Mass can also include such rituals as the **repudiation** of Christ, *the* **substitution** *of the* EUCHARIST *with bodily excretions,* and any number of **obscene rites** involving the *HOST.*

The Church of Satan

Former circus performer ANTON LAVEY (d. 1979) achieved international **notoriety** *when he founded the Church of Satan in San Francisco, California,* on Mayday Eve, 1966. With his *BLACK ATTIRE*, SHAVED HEAD, and *POINTED GOATEE BEARD*, he was so **persuasive** as the classic **seductive** Satanist that film director ROMAN POLANSKI cast him as the **devil** in *Rosemary's Baby* that same year. *His church was a* **success**, attracting several thousand CONVERTS, *including several Hollywood celebrities.*

LAVEY'S PHILOSOPHY

LAVEY **lapped up** all this publicity and was **careful** not to correct the more ERRONEOUS and LURID reports of the **sensation-hungry** tabloid press. Despite appearances, however, LAVEY was not a TRADITIONAL Satanist. *His PHILOSOPHY was based on* **secular materialism**. He believed in nothing other than the **here** and **now**. To LAVEY, *Satan was not the Antichrist,* because CHRIST himself was a *MYTH*. He saw Satan as a *PSYCHOLOGICAL ARCHETYPE*, a PROMETHEAN HERO trying to **free** himself from the **bonds** of *RELIGIOUS SUPERSTITION*, SOCIAL MORES, and the **repression** of natural *ANIMAL DRIVES*.

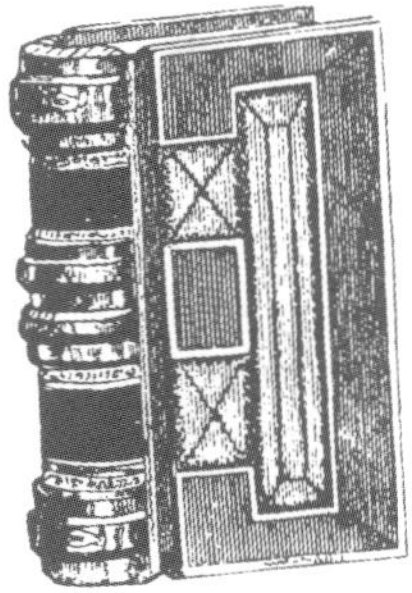

In *The Satanic Bible* (1969), LAVEY **declared** that humans were no more than highly evolved ANIMALS, *whose sole purpose was to* **procreate** *and* **enjoy** *their time on earth before the* ANNIHILATION *of DEATH*. Satan was the *IDEAL ARCHETYPE* for the **affirmation** of the SELF and the **pursuit** of PLEASURE. In this light, the *RITUALS* of the CHURCH of SATAN **functioned** more as PSYCHODRAMAS for individuals seeking LIBERATION from *REPRESSION* than **malevolent magic**. Many of the church's ritual elements were based on descriptions in HUYSMANS' *Là-Bas*.

LAVEY'S DECLINE

LAVEY did have a MORAL CODE. He **encouraged** his followers to **obey** the LAW and **respect** the FREEDOMS of others. *He believed that* DRUGS *encouraged* ESCAPISM *and* **discouraged** *their use*. In many ways, LAVEY did society a favor by **secularizing** the devil and making him *more* HUMAN, *less* DIABOLICAL, and *less* FRIGHTENING. *MEMBERSHIP* of the church, *which had never exceeded several thousand*, **declined** after various SPLINTER SECTS broke away to seek more **traditional** forms of Satanism based on MAGIC and WITCHCRAFT.

Satanic Ritual Abuse

Satanic ritual abuse (SRA) is an **assault** on an individual that is part of a RITUAL performed in the **worship** of Satan. Such an assault may be *PHYSICAL, PSYCHOLOGICAL,* or *SEXUAL. During the 1980s SRA became an increasing public concern in the UNITED STATES*, and by the end of the decade **concern** had turned into a WIDESPREAD **moral panic**.

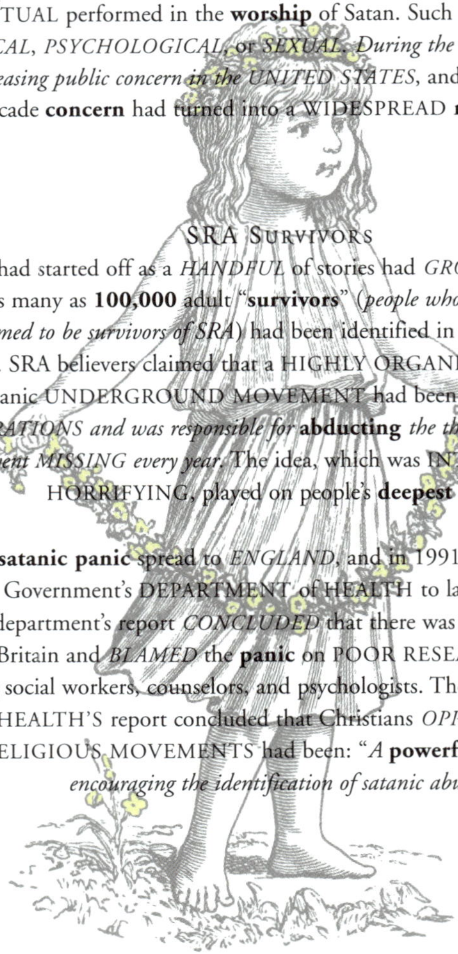

SRA Survivors

What had started off as a *HANDFUL* of stories had *GROWN* to the point where as many as **100,000** adult "**survivors**" (*people who believed themselves or claimed to be survivors of SRA*) had been identified in the United States alone. SRA believers claimed that a HIGHLY ORGANIZED worldwide satanic UNDERGROUND MOVEMENT had been operating for *GENERATIONS and was responsible for* **abducting** *the thousands of children who went MISSING every year.* The idea, which was INTOXICATINGLY HORRIFYING, played on people's **deepest fears**.

The **satanic panic** spread to *ENGLAND*, and in 1991, *SPURRED* the British Government's DEPARTMENT of HEALTH to launch an **inquiry**. The department's report *CONCLUDED* that there was **no evidence** for SRA in Britain and *BLAMED* the **panic** on POOR RESEARCH METHODS among social workers, counselors, and psychologists. The DEPARTMENT of HEALTH'S report concluded that Christians *OPPOSED* to new RELIGIOUS MOVEMENTS had been: "*A* **powerful influence** *encouraging the identification of satanic abuse.*"

In the United States, too, **no hard evidence** was found to support the claims being made. LAW ENFORCEMENT AGENCIES and PSYCHOLOGISTS debunked **SRA hysteria**. The PREVAILING VIEW is that the vast majority of SRA "**survivors**" were suffering from *FALSE MEMORY SYNDROME.* By the mid-1990s, **SRA mania** had all but disappeared.

Satanic Conspiracies

As with the *UFO ABDUCTION PHENOMENON*, thousands have **testified** that they have been **victims**, *but without presenting any* REAL EVIDENCE *to support their claims.* Believers in SATANIC CONSPIRACIES, however, have **answers** that neatly account for all OBJECTIONS—*if no evidence has yet been found, it is because the AUTHORITIES are also IMPLICATED in the* **conspiracy**. Sadly, the UNWITTING outcome of this MASS PROJECTION of misplaced **fears** and **anxieties** has been to WORSEN the condition of the **genuine victims** of trauma and nonritual forms of abuse. The only TANGIBLE result of the **SRA scandal** will be to encourage people to carry out **atrocities** and **abuse** in IMITATION of what they have read and seen in the media. For Satan, ALL PUBLICITY is *GOOD PUBLICITY.*

Defense Techniques

There are FEW GENUINE SATANISTS, *and most of them do not even believe in the* EXISTENCE *of* DEMONS. Those who do tend to be rebellious **delinquents** with a very **shallow** understanding of the *OCCULT*. As a result, Satanists represent very little **genuine threat** to SOCIETY. *Nevertheless, satanic ritual abuse does occasionally take place.* There have been several satanic **murders** in *NORWAY* over recent years, *COMMITTED* by followers of the "DEATH METAL" music scene. It is also possible that some of the **worst occult criminals** start off as Satanists.

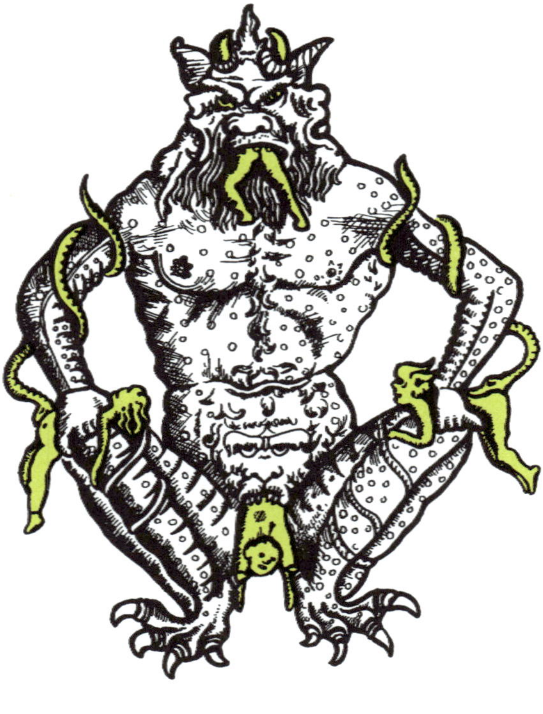

Protection from Satanic Attack

If you *SUSPECT* someone of being a Satanist and are *FEARFUL* of being **victimized**, the best thing you can do is to **avoid** his or her *COMPANY*. Do not let the person become AWARE of your **suspicions** *and take care not to* **irritate** *them or* **attract** *their* ATTENTION *in any way*. Satanists try to build up *POWERFUL EGOS* but can be extremely **sensitive** to any SUSPECTED SLIGHT. *Try to cast all consideration of such a person from your mind.* If you let them **haunt** your THOUGHTS, you can allow a "FEAR FORM" to grow inside you, *which can act as a* **repository** *for your* **unconscious fears** and grow into a *CANCER* of *ANXIETY*.

In such cases it may be necessary to **invoke** the "CHRIST ARCHETYPE" as the *ANTITHESIS* and *ANTAGONIST* of the "SATAN ARCHETYPE," which a powerful Satanist is able to project. *In this way even* **nonbelievers** *can* AVAIL *themselves of traditional* RELIGIOUS DEFENSES and discover that the name of JESUS CHRIST can be a powerful **shield**, *whether you believe in Him or not.* You can protect yourself and your home by using **amulets** (*see pages 144–155*), **holy water** (*see pages 186–187*), or **talismans** (*see pages 156–167*). In the extremely rare event that a Satanist is able to summon a demonic spirit to haunt or possess another person, **exorcism** may be called for (*see pages 178–185*).

Chapter 2

Black Lodges

The past **three centuries** have witnessed the emergence of many SECRET SOCIETIES, *or* BLACK LODGES, that have **espoused** occult beliefs. Many **black lodges** conceal themselves under the banner of FREEMASONRY, which claims **direct descent**, through the medieval order of the KNIGHTS TEMPLAR, to the builders of *SOLOMON'S TEMPLE* in Jerusalem.

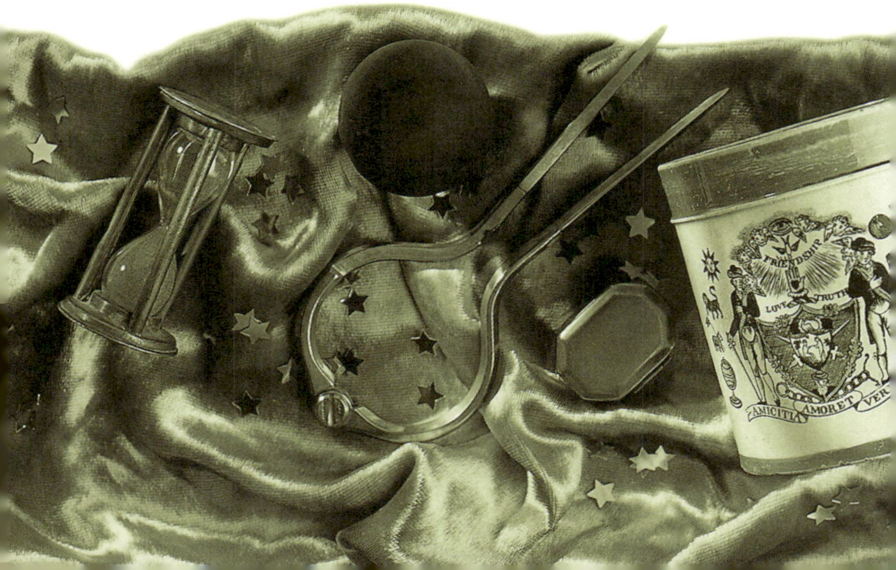

Secret Societies

The best-known secret societies include the Illuminati, the Freemasons, the Ordo Templi Orientis, and the Rosicrucians.

FREEMASONS AND ROSICRUCIANS

Freemasonry first appeared in *BRITAIN* in the middle of the 17th century. Two early masons were ELIAS ASHMOLE and ROBERT MORAY, *who were also* **founder members** *of the British Royal Society*, a highly respected **scientific body** whose early *PRESIDENTS* included ROBERT BOYLE and ISAAC NEWTON.

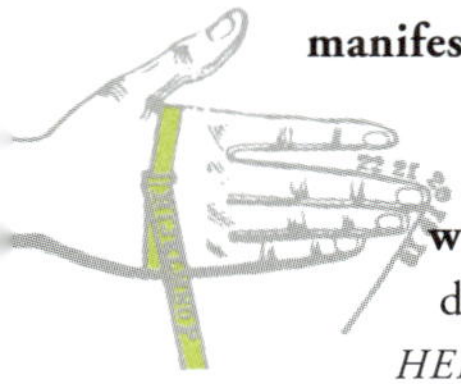

The first FREEMASONS were *INSPIRED* by the most **secret** and **mysterious** of all secret societies, the ROSICRUCIANS, whose extraordinary **manifestos** were published in *GERMANY* in the first quarter of the 17th century. The Rosicrucians promised to bring about a *universal reform of society and religion* that would unite the **warring faiths** and **nations** of the world under a new magical dispensation inspired by a **mystical philosophy** known as *HERMETIC NEOPLATONISM* and *SPIRITUAL ALCHEMY.*

The Rosicrucians' emphasis on FREEDOM, EQUALITY, and CHARITY influenced the **political beliefs** of the Freemasons, who were blamed for fomenting **revolutionary** movements against the old EUROPEAN MONARCHIES. Several of the leaders of the *AMERICAN REVOLUTION* were Freemasons, including GEORGE WASHINGTON, JAMES MADISON, and BENJAMIN FRANKLIN. This influence is still seen on the **dollar bill**, which bears the *MASONIC SYMBOL* of the **pyramid** topped by the ALL-SEEING EYE and the motto *novus ordo seclorum*, "the **new order** of the ages."

Renegade Societies

Although the ideals and mysticism of Rosicrucianism and Freemasonry are sound, both organizations have been exploited by less well-intentioned groups and individuals.

ILLUMINATI

In 1776 a *SECRET SOCIETY* called the ILLUMINATI was founded in *GERMANY.* Its members were promised **deep occult secrets** upon **initiation** into the *HIGHER RANKS* of the organization, *and it quickly attracted many* IDEALISTIC *young men of* **wealth** *and* **rank** *with its blend of* **philanthropy** *and* **mysticism**. The society's *FOUNDERS* were committed to nothing less than REVOLUTION and, *fearful of the reprisals that awaited them if the* AUTHORITIES *discovered them,* they attempted to **graft** themselves onto the FREEMASONS to STRENGTHEN their position.

The Freemasons were not slow to IDENTIFY these **interlopers** and set up a *CONFERENCE* to EXAMINE their beliefs. The Illuminati's leaders took part and attempted to take over the Freemasons. *They* FAILED *and shortly afterward were* **exposed** *to the authorities.* The society COLLAPSED but ILLUMINATI ideals spread throughout Europe, inspiring **intrigue** and **revolution**. *CONSPIRACY THEORIES* about the ILLUMINATI and FREEMASONS continue to *CIRCULATE* to this day. *Although there is no evidence that the* ILLUMINATI *practiced* **black magic**, there is some evidence that certain *MASONIC* or *QUASI-MASONIC LODGES* have ALIGNED themselves with **infernal forces** in order to ACHIEVE their AIMS.

Hierarchy

Freemasonry is **divided** into "*lodges*" that can be found in almost every country in the world. The Freemasons INSTITUTED a system of *INITIATORY DEGREES*, whereby members could **progress deeper** into the *INNER WORKINGS* and *BELIEFS* of the organization. These degrees **symbolize** the *LEVELS* through which we must PASS on our return to God. *The number of degrees VARIES in each of the orders.* The leading Masonic order, the UNITED GRAND LODGE, *uses the 33-DEGREE SYSTEM of the* ANCIENT *and* ACCEPTED RITE.

Freemasonry has provided an organizational model for most **esoteric** secret societies, including modern Rosicrucianism, neo-Templar orders, and **ceremonial** magic orders such as the HERMETIC ORDER of the GOLDEN DAWN and the ORDO TEMPLI ORIENTIS. The Masonic-style degree system, *or its equivalent,* has also been *WIDELY ADOPTED.*

The *LODGES* of these groups are **hierarchical**. *Elevation is achieved through a series of* INITIATIONS. The head of a lodge is usually called the *GRAND MASTER*, while new members are known as **neophytes**. *The low-level initiate or neophyte is* IGNORANT *of the more esoteric beliefs and practices of the organization and, therefore, of the* MOTIVATIONS *of its leaders.* Even well-intentioned people can thus find themselves **unwitting pawns** of malicious groups or individuals who have **hijacked** a lodge for their own ends.

Masonic Order of the Golden Centurium

The most INFAMOUS of all *BLACK LODGES* was the FOGC .: **or** 99 .: Lodge. It was founded in Munich, Germany, in 1840 by a group of RICH and POWERFUL men *who intended to use* **demonic entities** *to obtain* **power** *and* **wealth** *for its MEMBERS.* In spite of its name, the lodge had nothing to do with real FREEMASONRY. Its THREE-GRADE INITIATION system was *PURELY SYMBOLIC as all secrets were given to members upon initiation.*

THE LODGE DEMON

The **principal secret** lay in the fact that the lodge was dedicated to an **arch-demon** of the sphere of *MARS* called ASMODEUS, probably under the alias of BARZABEL. *His services did not come free.* Every member was BOUND to the *LODGE DEMON* by **oaths** and **blood rituals**. The neophyte's **first task** was to LEARN the adoration rituals. The 99 male members had to FORFEIT their **souls** to the demon upon their **deaths**.

RITUAL SACRIFICE

Every five years the lodge had to admit a NEW MEMBER to provide the demon with a **fresh soul**. As the number of members was fixed at **99**, *if none of the members had DIED within the preceding five-year period,* an EXISTING MEMBER had to be selected by **ballot** for *DEATH.* In good democratic fashion, EVERYONE was included in the ballot. The only EXCEPTION was the *GRAND MASTER, who could call for a fresh ballot if he were unlucky enough to choose the* **black ball**. However, he could do this only TWICE before submitting to his **fate**.

Rituals and Magical Techniques

The lodge's principal rituals were drawn from classical "**grimoires**" of ceremonial magic, such as the *Grimorium Verum* and the *Key of Solomon.* Such texts are **instruction manuals** for the practice of SORCERY, *in particular the EVOCATION of* ELEMENTAL *and* DEMONIC SPIRITS *that are BOUND to provide their assistance through the use of* **names**, **sigils** (magic symbols), *and* **incantations**. A DEMON who was frequently invoked was BELPHEGOR. Both BARZABEL and BELPHEGOR have the *REPUTATION* of being extremely *CLEVER, BRUTAL,* and *BLOODTHIRSTY.* If they agreed to work against someone, *the victim's PROSPECTS were* **grim**.

Death Rays

The FOGC's most *INFAMOUS* method of occult attack was "COMBAT TELEPATHY" *using an electrical instrument called a* **tepaphone**. For centuries, magicians and sorcerers have used **magic wands** equipped with **quartz** and **copper wire** as harmonic thought transmitters, *but the tepaphone developed the technology to a FIENDISH DEGREE.* Using an arrangement of *QUARTZ LENSES* and *COPPER COILS*, the device was able to manifest what has been called a PSYCHIC DEATH RAY. A **picture**, **hair**, or **personal object** belonging to the victim was placed under the **lens**, *while an ELECTRICAL CURRENT coursed through the* **coils**. The lodge members concentrated their *PSYCHIC ENERGIES* on the **lens** and **victim**. The tepaphone used extremely LOW-FREQUENCY VIBRATIONS that were *AMPLIFIED* and *PROJECTED* by psychic energy. The energy transmitted by the tepaphone acted as a form of "*remote poisoning*" on the victim, undermining the **autonomic nervous system** and leading to death by **heart attack**.

Material Criminality

The **horrors** that can be PERPETRATED by the members of a BLACK LODGE are *TERRIFYING*, but for the most part the CRIMES they commit have more in common with those of the *MAFIA* than *DIABOLISM*. BLACKMAIL, EXTORTION, and SEXUAL ABUSE are far more likely activities. If you are considering joining an **occult group**, *it is wise to discover as much about the* ORGANIZATION *and its* LEADERS *as possible.* Remember that lodges of ostensibly PHILANTHROPIC organizations like the **Freemasons** can be CORRUPTED from within.

GLAMOUR

For those who are DRAWN to them, the occult and its PRACTITIONERS can appear very *GLAMOROUS. A person claiming to be an* **adept** *has a special APPEAL and it is all too natural for some to* EXPLOIT *the opportunity to* INDULGE *their* **vanity** *and* **desires**. Even well-intentioned adepts can soon become SEXUAL PREDATORS if they find the *GAME* all too easy to play.

Self-protection

The best **defense** against a BLACK LODGE is to have *NOTHING* to do with it or its members. If you are not ENTIRELY sure of their **motives**, *do not join them.* Some occult groups DEMAND large amounts of **money** from new members, or ask them to make PROVISION for the group in their **wills**. This is a **bad** sign. The *STRENGTH* of an ESOTERIC GROUP rests on the *SPIRITUAL* not the *MATERIAL* plane. If you find yourself the victim of any form of **blackmail** or **threat**, go to the POLICE at once. *Do not on any account allow yourself to be intimidated into COMPLIANCE or you will most likely be further victimized.* BLACKMAIL is a much more *SERIOUS* crime than *ANYTHING* you are likely to want to keep HIDDEN.

If you want to LEAVE an occult group, JUST DO IT. A **corrupt** group has far more to fear from *EXPOSURE* than they have from losing one member. As for **binding oaths**, *REMEMBER* that a **contract** agreed to under *THREAT* is NOT **legally binding**. You do not necessarily have to BREAK a bond of **secrecy** in order to PROTECT yourself from **harm**.

Chapter 3
BLACK MAGIC

The **malicious** *USE* and *ABUSE* of occult powers is often described as BLACK MAGIC. However, in the context of the DARK ARTS as a whole, **black magic** involves the coercion of DEMONIC or ELEMENTAL spirits to carry out a *SORCERER'S* or *NECROMANCER'S* **will**.

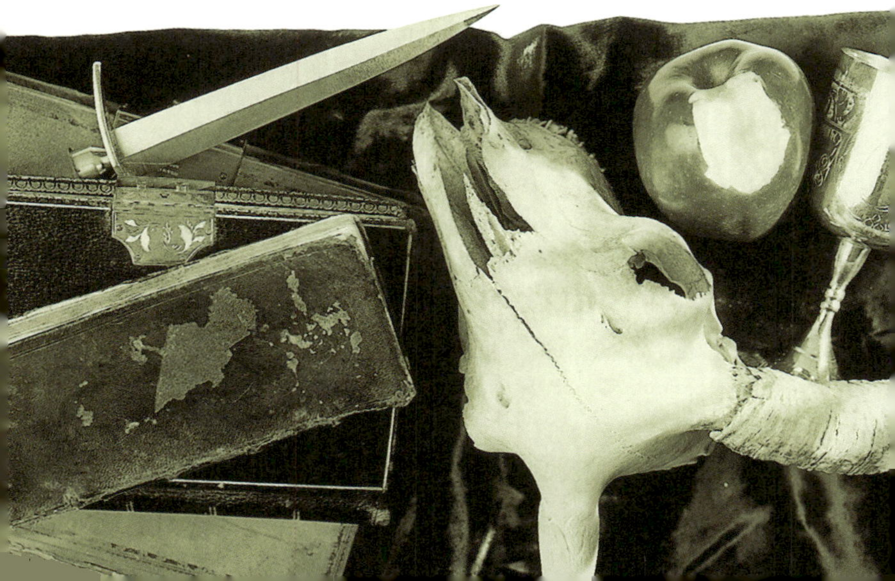

Definitions

Black magic, sorcery, and necromancy are often taken to be interchangeable terms in the context of European ritual magic. Both sorcerers and necromancers have humble origins as mere fortune-tellers.

SORCERY

The word sorcery is **derived** from the LATIN word *sortiarius*, which means "*caster of lots.*" The original sorcerer was little more than a person who used LOW MAGIC in the form of *BASIC DIVINATION* to **predict** the FUTURE. The term has come to have more *IMPRESSIVE CONNOTATIONS* and denotes **someone who practices magic**, *particularly black magic*, in order to bring about *SUPERNATURAL EFFECTS* on the material plane of existence.

NECROMANCY

The word necromancy has *TWO DERIVATIONS*. The first comes from the ANCIENT GREEK word *nekromanteia*, which means *the art of divination by using corpses.* Later *NEKROMANTEIA* was replaced by the LATIN *nigromantia*, from *niger*, meaning **black**. By combining these two words, we can derive the following definition: **necromancy is the Black Art of using corpses**, *or the spirits of the dead*, **in order to predict the future**.

We now think of a NECROMANCER as someone who **invokes** spirits, usually of the *SUB-ANGELIC* variety but not necessarily GHOSTS, in order to obtain **occult powers**. In TOLKIEN'S *Lord of the Rings*, SAURON, the embodiment of **evil**, is referred to as the DARK LORD or the NECROMANCER. Today, someone who wants his or her fortune told **consults** an ASTROLOGER, a PSYCHIC, or a MEDIUM. *SORCERERS and NECROMANCERS have* **darker** *things to do.*

The Left-hand Path

The MAGICIAN believes in a **hierarchical** universe, in which the EARTH is the *LOWEST* and most *MATERIAL* level. The EARTH is the realm of the *BODY, while the* HIGHER LEVELS *are the realms of SPIRIT*. Knowing that, as HERMES TRISMEGISTUS, the patron of magic, tells us, "*Whatever is ABOVE is like that which is BELOW; and whatever is BELOW is like that which is ABOVE*," the magician is aware of **correspondences** and **similarities** between *ALL* the levels of existence. He knows that the levels **mirror** each other, *and that when effects are made on one level*, there is a RIPPLE EFFECT on all levels.

What distinguishes *WHITE* from *BLACK MAGIC* is the **intention** behind it. The **intent** of the white magician, or THEURGIST, is to use his or her occult knowledge to **align** the *EARTHLY* with the *DIVINE*, in order that "*Thy will be done on earth, as it is in heaven.*" The black magician, on the other hand, **seeks to exploit** the higher powers to gain WEALTH and INFLUENCE in the material world. Those who **seize** power from above to rule below have no interest in aligning themselves with the DIVINE WILL. This **inferior** sort of magic is often referred to in **esoteric terminology** as the *LEFT-HAND PATH*. The Latin for LEFT is **sinister**, *and that is an apt description of many who walk that path.*

The Esoteric Tradition

All the higher forms of *WESTERN MAGIC* are rooted in the *ancient and universal tradition* known as the **Perennial Philosophy**. Its oldest forms are found in ANCIENT EGYPT and VEDIC INDIA. It **encapsulates** the belief that the **whole of creation** is of *DIVINE ORIGIN and is imbued with the DIVINE SPARK.* Furthermore, it holds that the hierarchies of creation are **sustained** by *SPIRITUAL ENTITIES*, and that divine wisdom and powers—*even union with the divine*—are within the reach of humankind.

Traces of the *PERENNIAL PHILOSOPHY* can be found in the beliefs of peoples all over the world. It imbues the *HIGHER TEACHINGS* and *MYSTICAL CURRENTS* of all the great religions, including *CHRISTIANITY, JUDAISM, HINDUISM*, and *ISLAM*. The more esoteric aspects of this ancient knowledge were first brought to *EUROPE* and from there to the *NEW WORLD* by a **chain of transmission** stretching from ANCIENT EGYPT, CLASSICAL GREECE, ROMAN ALEXANDRIA, and MOORISH SPAIN. The key sources of this **primordial understanding** include the writings of PLATO, HERMES TRISMEGISTUS, and IAMBLICHUS.

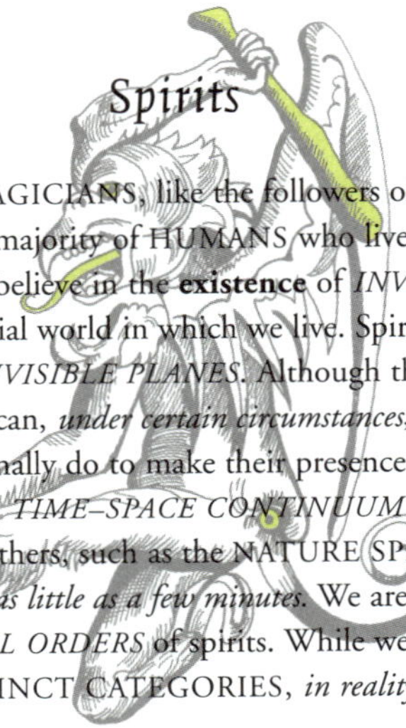

Spirits

SORCERERS and MAGICIANS, like the followers of the world's great religions and the vast majority of HUMANS who lived **before** our own MATERIALISTIC AGE, believe in the **existence** of *INVISIBLE SPIRITS* who **interact** with the material world in which we live. Spirits are **disincarnate entities** that exist on *INVISIBLE PLANES*. Although they lack MATERIAL FORM, many of them can, *under certain circumstances*, **become visible**—something they occasionally do to make their presence known to us. Most spirits exist outside the *TIME–SPACE CONTINUUM* and are, *in human terms*, **immortal**. Others, such as the NATURE SPIRITS known as **ephemera**, *exist for as little as a few minutes*. We are all familiar with several *PRINCIPAL ORDERS* of spirits. While we tend to think of them as DISTINCT CATEGORIES, *in reality they overlap.*

Angels

According to SEMITIC and VEDIC traditions, *angels were the first created beings*. As **spirits of light**, their function is to **reflect** the GLORY of the CREATOR and **sustain** all creation. They represent the IDEAS and INTELLIGENCES behind all forms.

Demons

In the Semitic tradition, demons are **fallen angels** *who refused to surrender their free will and* **rebelled** *against the* CREATOR, thereby **forfeiting** most of their **light** and being **excluded** from participating in the processes of creation.

Ghosts

Ghosts are the SPIRITS of the DEAD who exist on the **astral plane**—*the invisible fourth dimension of our own material plane*. They are spirits in **limbo**, who have yet to proceed to the next stage in the *CYCLE* of LIFE, DEATH, and REBIRTH. The most *COMMON CAUSE* for spirits to remain in limbo is that **they have not come to terms** with their own PHYSICAL DEATH.

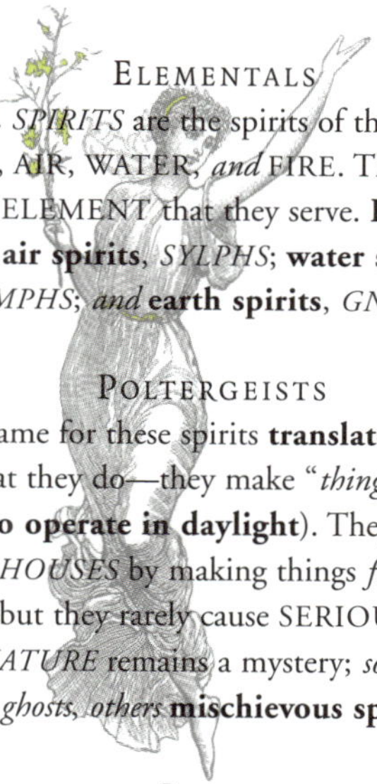

Elementals

The *ELEMENTAL SPIRITS* are the spirits of the **four philosophical elements**—EARTH, AIR, WATER, *and* FIRE. They are composed of the ESSENCE of the ELEMENT that they serve. **Fire spirits** *are called SALAMANDERS*; **air spirits**, *SYLPHS*; **water spirits**, *UNDINES or NYMPHS*; *and* **earth spirits**, *GNOMES*.

Poltergeists

The GERMAN name for these spirits **translates** as "*rattling ghosts,*" which is exactly what they do—they make "*things go bump in the night*" (**although they also operate in daylight**). They can cause a great deal of damage inside *HOUSES* by making things *fly through the air* and *crash to the ground*, but they rarely cause SERIOUS INJURY to humans. Their *EXACT NATURE* remains a mystery; *some consider them to be ghosts, others* **mischievous sprites**.

Devas

Devas are the *RULING NATURE SPIRITS*, ANGELIC ENTITIES that **govern** all the PHENOMENA of NATURE, particularly the forms of the **animal** and **plant kingdoms**.

Nature Spirits

The **lower nature spirits** are governed by the DEVAS. They tend to individual life forms. Among the most familiar are the DRYADS (*tree spirits*) and *FLOWER FAIRIES*.

Fairy Tribes

The "**little people**" *of folklore*—ELVES, BROWNIES, GOBLINS, DWARFS, and SPRITES—are classified either as *LOWER ANGELIC, SEMI-DEMONIC ENTITIES*, or as NATURE SPIRITS. They inhabit the **astral plane** that lies just beyond the limits of our **sensory perception**.

Heaven and Hell

The **great faiths** of the world share a conception of a *HEAVEN* or *PARADISE*, populated with *ANGELIC BEINGS* of *LIGHT* who are **devoted** to the adoration of the CREATOR. *The* ANTITHESIS *of* HEAVEN *is* HELL—**a world of darkness and evil**—populated by DEMONS whose **sole purpose** is the **seduction** of humanity from the PATH of LIGHT and its **ultimate destruction**.

THE WAR IN HEAVEN

According to the Semitic tradition, *the* CREATOR *granted the angels free will at the moment of their creation.* The majority **voluntarily** gave up this gift in *ADORATION* of their CREATOR, but one angel—the ARCHANGEL LUCIFER—entertained thoughts of **rebellion**. In certain traditions, LUCIFER was the very first created being. Overcome by **pride**, *he became* **jealous** *of the* CREATOR'S *authority.*

When the CREATOR ordered the angels to **bow down** before humanity, *his latest and favorite creation*, LUCIFER *rebelled*, taking a great host of angels with him. LUCIFER *and the* FAITHFUL ANGELS *under the leadership of* MICHAEL *fought the great War in Heaven.* When the rebel angels were **defeated**, they were **deprived** of their LIGHT but not of all their POWERS. They were cast into the PIT of HELL, *where they were turned into* **devils**, **fiends**, *and* **demons**. The traditional belief that demons were once angels appears to be universal and is not specific to the Semitic religions.

ADAM AND EVE

The fallen angels are **devoted** to the DESTRUCTION of all CREATION. *Their main target is humanity*, which they see as the PINNACLE of **evolved consciousness** on the earthly plane. It was LUCIFER, *in his incarnation as the worm Satan*, who **engineered** the FALL of HUMANITY. After their creation, ADAM and EVE **lived in innocence** in the GARDEN of EDEN. The CREATOR had given them **mastery** of all the world, but had **forbidden** them only one thing: *the fruit of the TREE of KNOWLEDGE*. SATAN—**the once mighty** LUCIFER—in the shape of a SERPENT tempted EVE to taste the FORBIDDEN FRUIT. *She was tempted and she gave the fruit to* ADAM *to eat*, **who also fell from grace**.

The story of ADAM and EVE is *SYMBOLIC* of how we became **separated** from the DIVINE SOURCE and prey to TEMPTATION. Every human soul is a **battleground** for the forces of LIGHT and DARKNESS, *good and evil*. The agenda of SATAN and his *FALLEN ANGELS* is to **corrupt** humanity by making us ever more **powerful** and **destructive** as a species, *and ever more* **degenerate** *and* **faithless** *as individuals*.

The Angelic Hierarchy

The faithful heavenly host still serves the light and sustains all creation. The angels are traditionally arranged into a hierarchy of orders known in Christian angelology as choirs. According to the Christian mystic Dionysius, there are nine angelic choirs.

SERAPHIM

The HIGHEST ORDER of angels is that of the **mighty** Seraphim, the *CHIOTH HA QADESH* of the KABBALAH, the "*Holy Living Creatures*" who are the **closest** to the *DIVINE SOURCE* and **radiate an inconceivable magnitude of light**. They exist above the realm of the planets.

CHERUBIM

Next are the Cherubim, "*the whirling forces*" who receive their LIGHT from the *SERAPHIM* and **reflect divine knowledge and wisdom**. They, too, exist beyond the *PLANETARY SPHERE*.

THRONES

These are the "*many-eyed wheels of fire*" or the "*strong and mighty ones*" who **circle** the divine source, reflecting the **power** and the **glory** of the THRONE.

Dominions

The "*brilliant ones*" exist at the level where the SPIRITUAL and PHYSICAL PLANES **merge**. They reflect the desire to **transcend** the LIMITATIONS of the *MATERIAL PLANE.*

Virtues

The "*flaming ones*" are the **awe-inspiring** avenging angels. They govern all NATURAL LAWS and inspire **virtue** and **valor**.

Powers

These angels **guard** the PATHWAYS to *HEAVEN* and **defend** *the manifest universe against the DESTRUCTIVENESS of demons*. Their light inspires **devotion** to good over evil.

Principalities

This is the first **angelic choir** that is able to **intervene actively** in the *AFFAIRS* of *HUMANITY.* They guide GOVERNMENTS and LEADERS and inspire **responsibility** in individuals.

Archangels

The **mighty archangels** are the angels that appear occasionally as *GREAT WINGED BEINGS* of *LIGHT*. They are the **herald angels** who deliver the word of GOD on EARTH.

Angels

The lowest choir of angels is directly involved in **assisting** *humanity.* These are the **guardian angels**, who CANNOT interfere with our own *FREE WILL*, but can **guide** us on the PATH of TRUTH. *This order of angels works overtime* **preventing** *ACCIDENTS and DISASTERS.*

The Demonic Hierarchy

Medieval and Renaissance scholars compiled the main lists of demons, which display a strong anti-pagan bias. The magus Francis Barrett classified the infernal hordes into nine orders, reflecting Dionysius's nine angelic choirs.

False Gods

These most POWERFUL of DEMONS seek to **usurp** the name of GOD and **crave** to be worshipped in his place. BEELZEBUB is among their number.

Spirits of Lies

These are the **fiends** behind all *FALSE PROPHETS* and *ORACLES*. The **serpent** PYTHO is their *PRINCE*.

Vessels of Iniquity

The *EVIL GENIUSES* led by BELIAL **invent all the vices** that *lead humanity astray.*

Revengers of Evil

Led by ASMODEUS, *these demons inspire humans to* **pass judgment** on one another.

Deluders

The "*cunning ones*" **imitate** MIRACLES and **aid** CONJURERS and WITCHES, inspiring *FALSE PROPHETS* and *FALSE MESSIAHS*.

Aerial Powers

These demons, led by MERIRIM, cause DISEASE by **corrupting** the air *and help witches* **destroy crops** *and* **blight orchards**.

Furies

These are the powers of EVIL, DISCORDS, WAR, and DEVASTATION, which promote **jealousy** and **cynicism**. They are led by ABADDON, the DESTROYER.

Accusers

Also known as the "*Inquisitors*," this **horde** is led by ASTAROTH, known in GREEK as *DIABALOS*, which means "*accuser*" or "*calumniator*."

Tempters and Ensnarers

These are the **counterparts** of the guardian angels—*the devils in each one of us*. Their *PRINCE* is MAMMON.

Invoking Spirits

One of the *KEY ELEMENTS* of magic is the performance of rituals to **summon** spirits. A spirit from any ORDER can be invoked, *as long as the correct ritual is performed.* Spirits can also be **evoked**, which means that they can be **forced to become manifest** on the MATERIAL PLANE. This is achieved when their *TRUE NAMES* are *SPOKEN. In practice, however, it is extremely* **dangerous** *to evoke the higher angels and more powerful demons* because their presence can be **overwhelming**. *Needless to say,* practitioners of *BLACK MAGIC* summon the POWERS of DARKNESS instead of the FORCES of LIGHT.

Summoning Ritual

Sorcerers aim to bind *LESSER DEMONS* and *ELEMENTALS* to carry out their will. The first element of the summoning ritual is to **draw a magic circle**. *The circle protects sorcerers from being attacked by the spirits that they summon.* Facing EAST, the sorcerer will draw a **protective pentagram** in the air with a **wand** or **dagger**, and then, as a rule, *he or she will invoke the name of the ELEMENTAL KING of the* AIR. The sorcerer **repeats** this procedure *facing the remaining THREE POINTS of the COMPASS,* invoking the ELEMENTAL KINGS of FIRE to the south, WATER to the west, and EARTH to the north. *Then, while burning* **noxious incense**, the sorcerer invokes and binds the chosen spirit. To secure the spirit's cooperation, it may be necessary to offer it a **blood sacrifice** *or some equally BARBAROUS offering.*

Subjugating the Spirits

It is *IRONIC* that a sorcerer will often seek to **control** the spirit by invoking **holy names**: "*I command you in the name of the* ALMIGHTY *and His only begotten son* JESUS CHRIST." Many magicians are convinced that they may LEGITIMATELY invoke the *GREAT ARCHANGELS* of the *FOUR DIRECTIONS* when creating a **magic circle** and entreat them for their **protection** *while summoning a demonic or elemental spirit.* Certain magical traditions hold that it is our right as humans to **subjugate** lesser spirits to our will *as long as our intent is* **pure**. However, it is a little difficult to imagine what *GOOD* demons are capable of, *given their* EVIL NATURES.

Avoiding Trouble

Unlike WITCHES and SATANISTS who come together in **covens** and **lodges**, SORCERERS, NECROMANCERS, and other PRACTITIONERS of the DARK ARTS usually work alone. Your best **defense** against such persons is to **avoid all contact** with them. When avoidance is impossible, make sure you show the *SUSPECT PERSON* all due **courtesy**, *while drawing as little attention to yourself as possible.* Practitioners of **black magic** often have very **sensitive egos** and are **easily offended**. *They should, therefore, be treated with respect* and under no circumstances be shown up in front of others.

PRACTICAL ADVICE

Make whatever EXCUSES you need not to receive them in your home and **never accept an invitation to theirs**. *NEVER* accept **food** or **drink** from them, as they may have **tampered** with them *in ways that might establish a PSYCHIC LINK between you.* For the same reason, *never accept a* **gift** *from such a person.*

When CHRIST declared that we should **love our enemies**, he did not exclude **sorcerers** and other **practitioners** of the *DARK ARTS*. If you suspect someone of being a NECROMANCER, do not be tempted by the TEMPTER and ACCUSER DEMONS into passing **judgment**. REMEMBER: "*Vengeance is Mine,*" *SAYETH THE LORD.*

Defense Techniques

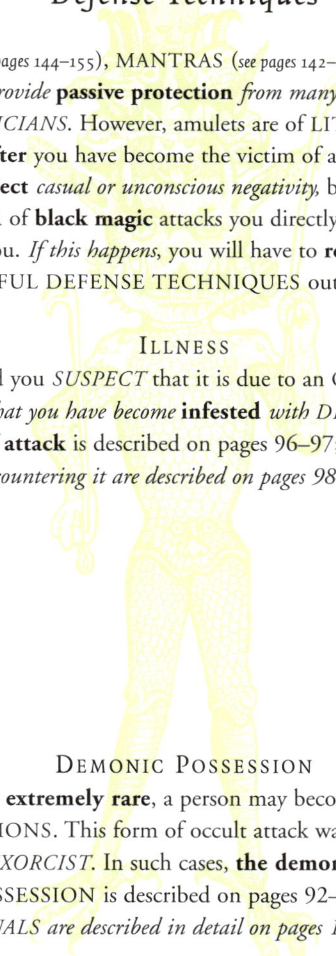

AMULETS (*see pages 144–155*), MANTRAS (*see pages 142–143*), and PRAYERS (*see page 135*) *will provide* **passive protection** *from many forms of molestation by BLACK MAGICIANS.* However, amulets are of LITTLE ASSISTANCE if you use them **after** you have become the victim of an *OCCULT ATTACK. Amulets can* **deflect** *casual or unconscious negativity,* but if a POWERFUL PRACTITIONER of **black magic** attacks you directly, they will not always PROTECT you. *If this happens,* you will have to **resort** to the more POWERFUL DEFENSE TECHNIQUES outlined below.

Illness

If you fall **ill** and you *SUSPECT* that it is due to an OCCULT ATTACK, *it is possible that you have become* **infested** *with DISEASE SPIRITS.* This form of **attack** is described on pages 96–97; *effective ways of countering it are described on pages 98–99.*

Demonic Possession

Although it is **extremely rare**, a person may become **possessed** by POWERFUL DEMONS. This form of occult attack was accurately portrayed in the film *THE EXORCIST*. In such cases, **the demon must be exorcised.** DEMONIC POSSESSION is described on pages 92–99 and *EXORCISM RITUALS are described in detail on pages 178–187.*

Chapter 4
WITCHCRAFT

Witchcraft is not, in itself, a **Dark Art**. Many of the witches *PERSECUTED* in centuries past may have been practitioners of a form of NATURE-WORSHIPPING MAGIC or merely HERBAL HEALERS, rather than the *DEVIL WORSHIPPERS* that their accusers claimed them to be. However, *like any form of magic*, witchcraft can be, and **frequently** is, abused.

Western Witchcraft

The **history** of witchcraft in EUROPE and NORTH AMERICA has been completely *REWRITTEN* during the past century. It is now **fashionable** to portray the many thousands who perished during witch-hunts between the 15th and 18th centuries as the *innocent victims of religious and civil persecution.* There is no doubt that a great many of them were WRONGLY ACCUSED. However, **it should not be underestimated** *how much serious MISCHIEF witchcraft can cause in the wrong hands.* There are many different forms of witchcraft practiced throughout the world, *but the main ingredients of* **malicious** *witchcraft everywhere are* SPITE, ENVY, belief in *SUPERNATURAL POWERS*, and various techniques for focusing and projecting **ill will**.

THE BURNING TIMES

The terrible medieval **witch-hunts**, known as the "*Burning Times,*" which led to the deaths of many thousands, *began at the end of the 15th century and continued intermittently for the next 300 years.* The persecution of witchcraft was INITIATED in the year 1484 when POPE INNOCENT VIII issued a **Papal Bull** redefining witchcraft, *hitherto considered a remnant of pagan SUPERSTITION and not an evil CULT*, as Satanism— the WORSHIP of the DEVIL. This reversed the earlier legal doctrine outlined in the widely disseminated 10th-century ecclesiastical document, the *CANON EPISCOPI*, that stated that a **belief** in witchcraft rather than its practice was **heretical**. Until the 15th century, *people who claimed to be witches were considered to be* MAD *or* DELUDED.

The Hammer of the Witches

Two years after the Papal Bull had **demonized** witches as Satanists, *two German inquisitors,* HEINRICH KRAMER *and* JACOB SPRENGER, *who had been delegated to purge the* GERMAN *lands of witchcraft,* published a professional **manual** for witch-hunters called the *MALLEUS MALEFICARUM* (*The Hammer of the Witches*).

The *MALLEUS* proved to be one of the most influential books of early legal history. It went through **30 editions** between 1486 and 1669, and was widely distributed. In 1948 the English translator REVEREND MONTAGUE SUMMERS wrote: "*The MALLEUS lay on the bench of every JUDGE, the desk of every MAGISTRATE. It was the ultimate, irrefutable, unarguable AUTHORITY. It was implicitly accepted not only by Catholic but also by Protestant legislature. It is not too much to say that the MALLEUS MALEFICARUM is among the most important, wisest, and weightiest books of the world.*"

Devil Worshippers

While few people today would wholeheartedly agree with the good reverend's assessment, *it is undeniable that the MALLEUS was enormously influential.* It is very hard to say with any certainty how much of it was true and how much was the product of the authors' **fevered**, if not to say *PARANOID*, **imaginations**. *However, few dared to question its validity at the time.* There were two good reasons for this. First, the CHURCH considered it **heretical** for anyone to DISPUTE the reality of witchcraft as laid down by the *MALLEUS*; and second, because in the late 15th century most people *BELIEVED* in the reality of witchcraft. *Evidence of it was found in every country and it was greatly FEARED.*

What the *MALLEUS* did was to **ally** witches with the Christian devil, while confirming **paranoia** about a universal **conspiracy** of Satanists. *Witches were no longer malevolent lone operators.* They now ranked with SORCERERS and NECROMANCERS as an organized **menace** to Christendom and card-carrying *DEVIL WORSHIPPERS* flying on **broomsticks** to attend satanic **orgies** and commune with the PRINCE of DARKNESS himself. *The obvious* **misogyny** *of the MALLEUS created the enduring image of the witch as an OLD, UGLY HAG.*

CONVICTION AND TORTURE

The *MALLEUS* was divided into three sections: *the* **first** *was a DIATRIBE against witchcraft and diabolism*; the **second** minutely DESCRIBED the practices of witchcraft; *and the* **third** *laid down the legal rules for* CONVICTING *witches.* This last section described exactly what *CONFESSIONS* should be *EXTRACTED* from the accused and how. *Its procedures ensured that anyone ARRESTED stood very little chance of ESCAPE* and were responsible for **appalling tortures** and many hundreds, *if not thousands*, of **judicial murders**.

Bad Magic

The *MALLEUS MALEFICARUM* lists a great variety of **vicious** techniques supposedly used by witches to cause **harm**. *Although they are too numerous to list in full,* here are a few examples.

Effigies

An ancient and universal technique of malicious witchcraft is the preparation of an effigy—*usually made of WAX to which the intended victim's* **hair** *or* **nail clippings** *have been added.* This is sometimes made in the CRUDE LIKENESS of the VICTIM. The effigy or "*poppet*" is then subjected to certain treatments, *such as immersion in water to induce* **drowning**, or **burning** to cause death from **fever** or in a **fire**.

Spell of the Black Hen

A well-known example of effigy magic involves stuffing the likeness of a **black hen** with SHREDS *of the intended victim's CLOTHING and/or HAIR.* The effigy is then stuck with **black pins** and *DROWNED*, *BURIED*, or *BURNED.*

Spells and Hexes

Spells and curses, often called **hexes** in witchcraft, are **spoken** or **written formulas** capable of achieving supernatural effects. *A belief in the MAGICAL POWER of the SPOKEN WORD is inherent in all cultures prior to the modern age.* Although we seldom acknowledge the fact, words are indeed magical. They **conjure up** images in the mind's eye. To speak somebody's **name** is to bring them immediately to mind; *to have some essential part of them present, as it were,* and available for us to *PROJECT* our *IDEAS* onto.

The WRITTEN WORD, too, has always been considered magical, being an arrangement of **cryptic symbols** *that somehow corresponds to the intimate reality of things.* Among the pagan GERMANIC tribes of the early CHRISTIAN era, **runes** (*ancient northern European letters*) were considered inherently magical, and those who knew how to use them were credited with having **special powers**. *Writing is a magical art that is now so widely practiced that it appears MUNDANE.*

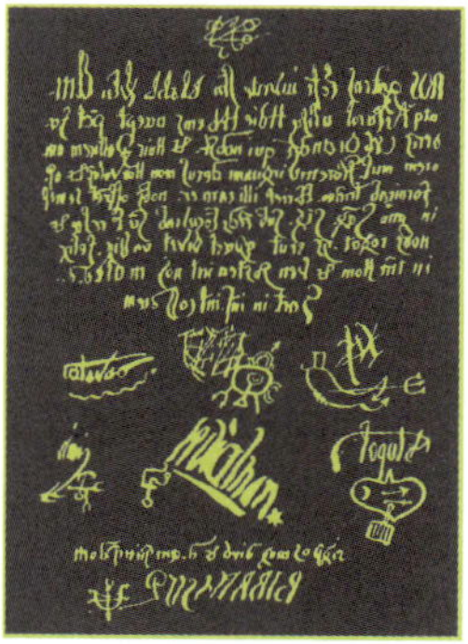

THE EFFICACY OF ANY HEX OR SPELL IS DEPENDENT ON TWO THINGS:

1. *The words must have a direct CORRESPONDENCE with the focus of the magician's intent.*

2. *The magician must have complete CONFIDENCE in the spell's inherent power to hit its target. The more the magician UNDERSTANDS INTUITIVELY just how a spell will work, the greater its chances of SUCCESS.*

For a more detailed explanation of the magical power inherent in words, *see pages 142–143.*

African Witchcraft

Although witchcraft is traditionally associated with MEDIEVAL EUROPE and COLONIAL AMERICA, *it exists on every CONTINENT and in every CULTURE.* The witches of AFRICA, the MIDDLE EAST, INDIA, and EAST ASIA may go under different names, but they share many of their techniques and beliefs with their Western counterparts. The AFRICAN continent is the **source** of many magical traditions and religions, including VODOU, OBEAH, JU-JU, and MUTI.

The Story of Adam

As with Western witchcraft, African witchcraft is not in itself a Dark Art. The story of ADAM, however, provides an example of its most **macabre** side and touches on many different elements of African witchcraft. *In 2001 the* **torso** *of a* YOUNG BOY *was found* **floating** *in the River Thames near Tower Bridge in London.* The body was that of a five-year-old boy whom the police called "ADAM." Advanced **forensic** techniques established that Adam had spent most of his life in southern NIGERIA and was most likely a member of the YORUBA people—*Nigeria's second largest ethnic group.* He had been brought to LONDON via GERMANY two weeks before his **ritual murder**. His throat had been cut, *and his body had been DRAINED of BLOOD before being dismembered.*

The medical examiner recovered the remains of a **calabar bean** from Adam's stomach. *Ground into a TASTELESS and COLORLESS POISON*, calabar causes **paralysis**, and is sometimes given to **suspected witches** and **sacrificial victims**. The murder was initially thought to be a ritual MUTI killing—*a South African RITE performed to obtain human body parts for "MEDICINE" and witchcraft.* However, certain indications (*too gruesome to detail here*) were not in keeping with what is known about MUTI customs.

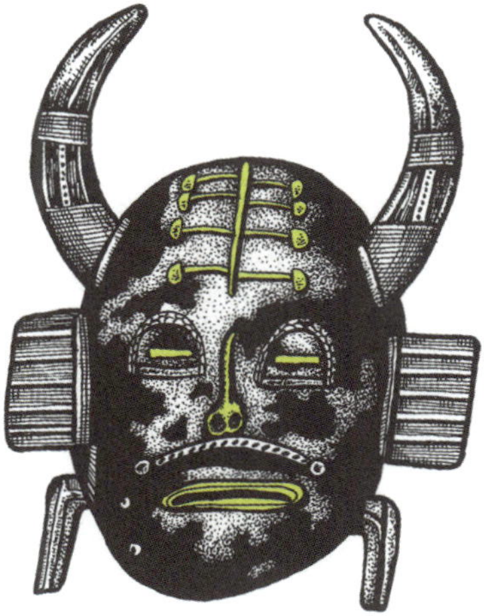

A SACRIFICE TO OCHUN

The **orange shorts** placed on ADAM 24 hours after his death provided another clue. The color orange is associated with OCHUN, one of the ORISHA or **ancestor gods** of the Yoruba people. OCHUN is the youngest of the ORISHAS and is known as "*the Mother of Secrets.*" She is regarded as an intermediary between the YORUBA and OLODUMARE, their supreme deity. *PRAYERS are unlikely to reach Olodumare without using Ochun as an INTERMEDIARY.*

CULTURAL and FORENSIC **clues** suggest that ADAM may have been sacrificed to OCHUN to speed prayers, *probably a petition for luck,* to OLODUMARE. Such **ritual killings** are abhorred by the YORUBA community and are quite **rare**, *but occasionally a group of people will* **conspire** *to perform a human sacrifice in order to ensure the SUCCESS of a BUSINESS or POLITICAL VENTURE.*

Asian Witchcraft

Throughout the vast regions of CENTRAL and EAST ASIA, magical traditions still thrive. *And where there's magic*, there is always witchcraft.

ISLAM

Much of ASIA, from the BOSPORUS to INDONESIA, is **Muslim**, and in all Islamic countries local magic has mixed with traditions from Islam's Arabian heartland. We are familiar with the elements of Arabian magic from the **fables** told in *THE ARABIAN NIGHTS*: *genies, flying carpets, and sorcerer-viziers*, but **Surah 113** of the KORAN (*which, no less than the BIBLE, is full of references to magic and the supernatural*) makes specific mention of witchcraft:

113:1 *Say: I seek refuge in (Allah) the Lord of the dawn,*
113:2 *From the evil of what He has created,*
113:3 *And from the evil of the utterly dark night when it comes,*
113:4 *And from the evil of witches who BLOW on KNOTS,*
113:5 *And from the evil of the envier when he envies.*

This reference to witches **blowing** on **knots** recalls an infamous hexing device used by European witches called the "*witches' ladder*"—a length of **string** tied with a series of **knots** containing a cursed black hen's **feather**. Some Muslims carry SURAH 113 as an **amulet** against witchcraft.

ISLAM has done little to undermine the traditional magic lore of MALAYSIA, *where SHAMANISM, ASTROLOGY, DIVINATION, OMENS, and other forms of sympathetic magic are common.* The MALAYS have adopted the Arabian belief in **genies**, and there is still a lively belief in many forms of witchcraft.

India

The LOWER CASTES and DRAVIDIAN peoples of India preserve a body of traditional witch lore that has much in common with European witchcraft. Witches are recognized by marks on their bodies; *they do not SINK in water*; they have animal familiars, usually **cats**, *whose form they can assume*; and they use **hair**, **teeth**, or **nail clippings** to gain power over people and make effigies of them out of WAX, CLAY, or DOUGH, *which they then* **torture**. The most feared witch in India is the **vampiric Ralaratri** ("*black night*"), *whose powers include SECOND SIGHT, the EVIL EYE, control of the WEATHER, and POTION MAKING.*

Tibet

TIBETAN BUDDHISM retains many magical beliefs from the native **Bon religion** that it replaced. Bon sorcerers were credited with amazing powers and greatly feared until recent times. *Even today, many Tibetans believe that witches can send DISEASE DEMONS to PLAGUE their victims.* In LADAKH, formerly part of western Tibet, folk healers known as ORACLES *appear to suck BLACK LUMPS and other objects from the stomachs of the sick*, while emitting FRIGHTFUL SHRIEKS to **exorcise** disease demons.

Wicca

Witchcraft is not to be confused with Wicca, *or NEO-PAGAN witchcraft*, which is a 20th-century phenomenon molded from a **romantic synthesis** of EUROPEAN PAGANISM, *HERMETIC MAGIC*, and BRITISH FOLKLORE. Many Wiccans believe that their religion can be equated with a pre-Christian "*Old Religion*," and that the persecuted witches of Europe were their **co-religionists**, *who had survived as an underground cult for a thousand years before the BURNING TIMES*. Most Wiccan elders no longer believe in these ENTICING but FANCIFUL IDEAS.

Wicca is the only world religion to have originated in England. GERALD GARDNER and a number of other English "*Old Religionists*" coined the name in the 1940s to DISTINGUISH their beliefs from *SATANISM* and *SORCERY*. Wicca has no **central authority** or **organizing body**, *although many Wiccans are members of umbrella groups such as the COVENANT of the GODDESS*. Estimates suggest that there might be as many as *ONE-HALF MILLION* to *TWO MILLION* Wiccans in NORTH AMERICA alone.

Beliefs and Rituals

Wicca is a **life-affirming**, **fertility-based** PAGAN RELIGION that, *because it has no sacred texts,* has no ORTHODOX set of beliefs. Most Wiccans believe in a dual deity, often referred to as "*the Lord and the Lady.*" *NATURE* is the *SUPREME CREATIVE FORCE* and most Wiccan rituals celebrate important dates in the calendar, such as MIDSUMMER, YULE, and BELTANE (*May Eve*), which they see as part of a **self-attunement** to the ELEMENTS and CYCLES of NATURE. One of the principal symbols of Wicca is the **pentagram**, *and Wiccans commonly perform a variant of the PENTAGRAM RITUAL* that is described on pages 172–175.

Magic

Wiccans have a **magical worldview** that emphasizes the *POWER* of *SPIRIT* and the GREAT GODDESS *as the personification of NATURE.* They tend to have a strong sense of **ecology** and work with the spirits of Nature to sustain the earth as a *LIVING PARADISE.* Wiccans use the same ritual tools as ceremonial magicians: the **cup**, **dagger**, **wand**, and **pantacle**, *with the addition of a CEREMONIAL SWORD called an* **athame**. AMULETS, TALISMANS, CHARMS, and HERBS are used magically as a part of spell-working. Wiccan ethics are summed up by the *WICCAN REDE*: "*An' it harm none, Do as ye will.*"

Witchcraft Today

OLD-FASHIONED WITCHCRAFT is as common today as it was in medieval times. However, it is usually only found in those parts of the world that have yet to become too Westernized, *that is to say, not yet* **subject** *to the MATERIALISTIC CULTURE of EUROPE and the UNITED STATES.* It is not religion that eradicates witchcraft, *but materialism and the* SOPHISTICATED SKEPTICISM *promoted by the modern mass media.* This is not to say that skepticism is a sure DEFENSE against **malicious** witchcraft. A DISBELIEVING Westerner traveling in the developing world, *particularly in RURAL districts where witchcraft is still prevalent,* is just as much at risk as the **superstitious** locals.

The Evil Eye

Belief in the "*evil eye*" is *ANCIENT* and *UNIVERSAL*. There is no culture on earth that has not been **bedeviled** by the idea that some people can, *just by letting their* **gaze** *fall upon another*, cause them to suffer ACCIDENT, DISEASE, or even DEATH. Some believe that only witches and sorcerers have this power, *while others believe that people with CROSSED EYES, a WALLEYE, or even CATARACTS* can consciously or unconsciously produce the same effects. There are some who believe that DEMONS can use a **damaged eye** as a **window** from which to project their evil. Whatever the case, it is true that a powerful malefactor, like a skilled **hypnotist**, *can establish a psychic link with a sufficiently PENETRATING glance*. Once the link has been established, the door is OPEN to ABUSE.

Universal Self-protection Techniques

The best forms of protection against harmful witchcraft are amulets and protective charms, the use of which goes back to prehistory.

Amulets

There are *TWO* kinds of amulet. *The first is a fetish*—a small OBJECT in which a PROTECTIVE SPIRIT resides. This is like housing your guardian angel in a **nut** *or some other small object that you then carry around with you.* The HUICHOL Native Americans of MEXICO believe that **crystals** contain *ANCESTOR SPIRITS. To find one is considered a great blessing* and treasured for the **luck** and **protection** it can bring.

The other, *and these days more common*, form of amulet is a **mascot** or **charm** that is carried or, more usually, *worn like* **jewelry** *as a protection against the evil eye and other hexes.* Common forms of amulet throughout the world include STONES, TEETH, CLAWS (*especially naturally shed* **cat's claws**), SHELLS, CORAL, and CRYSTALS. Prehistoric *ARROWHEADS* that have been found *in situ* are also favorite amulets. You can learn more about how to make and use **amulets** on pages 144–155.

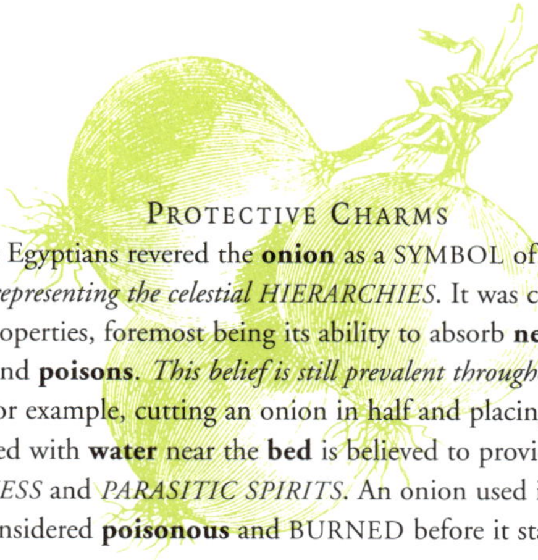

Protective Charms

The ancient Egyptians revered the **onion** as a SYMBOL of the UNIVERSE, *its LAYERS representing the celestial HIERARCHIES*. It was considered to have magical properties, foremost being its ability to absorb **negative energy**, **sickness**, and **poisons**. *This belief is still prevalent throughout the world.* In MEXICO, for example, cutting an onion in half and placing one half on top of a **glass** filled with **water** near the **bed** is believed to provide *PROTECTION* against *ILLNESS* and *PARASITIC SPIRITS*. An onion used in this way should be considered **poisonous** and BURNED before it starts to rot.

St. John's Wort

In every part of the world there are particular **plants** considered to be innately protective against evil. One such plant, *held sacred in every Christian country where it grows,* is ST. JOHN'S WORT (*Hypericum perforatum*). There is much religious symbolism pertaining to the plant. For example, its **branches**, when viewed from above, *make the shape of a* CROSS; and it exudes *BLOOD-RED OIL* from its **flowers**. In magical lore it is governed by the **Sun** and enhances the inner light of the soul when taken *MEDICINALLY*. The red oil is wonderfully *CURATIVE* when applied to BLISTERS, BURNS, CUTS, and BRUISES. *The plant is traditionally HUNG UP in the home to PREVENT witches from ENTERING in any form.*

Chapter 5
Vodou

Voodoo, or Vodou as it is more correctly spelled in CREOLE, has suffered from extremely **bad press** in the WEST. *It is actually a VIBRANT RELIGION rather than one of the Dark Arts*, but it is included here because it throws much light on the **occult**, while its **sorcery** is so feared that it merits consideration within its CULTURAL CONTEXT.

A Brief History of Vodou

Vodou is an AFRO-CARIBBEAN **religion** that appeared in HAITI on the island of HISPANIOLA. *During the early 19th century, it migrated to the* UNITED STATES *via* NEW ORLEANS. *SUPPRESSED, but never EXTERMINATED*, it survives today and has **increased in popularity** over recent years.

Between 1510 and 1830 some three million **slaves** were brought to HAITI from WEST AFRICA. *Those who* **escaped** *the plantations fled to the hill country*, where they made contact with the few surviving TAINO NATIVE AMERICANS and other escaped slaves. The Native American and African fugitives (*known as maroons*) shared many beliefs and rituals. *Both REVERED ancestral spirit deities* (*lwa*), whom they propitiated through **animal sacrifices** and communed with through ritual **drumming** and collective **dancing**. *THE AFRICANS brought with them a pantheon of deities called RADA.* The NATIVE AMERICANS had their own deities that, *like those of the AZTECS and MAYANS*, were more **violent** than their African counterparts.

Fusion of Beliefs

Out of this fusion grew a **new pantheon** of *LWA* called *PETWO*. Vodou venerated both the *RADA* and the *PETWO* deities, *but it was the Petwo that gave Vodou its spirit of* **revolt**. The new beliefs filtered into the SLAVE CAMPS and, although the African slaves came from at least 40 different peoples, *Vodou became a powerful UNIFYING FORCE*. So powerful, in fact, that it inspired a **13-year rebellion** that culminated in HAITI becoming **the first black nation** to achieve **independence** from COLONIAL RULE in 1804.

Dancing, Drumming, and Possession

The PHENOMENON of POSSESSION is one of the most **fascinating** and **unusual** aspects of Vodou. Possession regularly occurs during **worship** led by the OUNGAN and MANBO (*priest and priestess*). Possession is facilitated by **singing**, **drumming**, and **dancing**, after the preparatory rituals have been observed. *It is the DANCERS who are possessed.* The various *LWA* respond to different SONGS, DRUMS, and RHYTHMS. *A dancer who has completely* **surrendered** *to the drumming may receive the BLESSING of possession.* Once the dancer is possessed, the IDENTITY of the SPIRIT can easily be recognized from the movements that the dancer executes. *During possession the dancer is completely* **entranced**. Afterward he or she will be **exhausted** but otherwise **unharmed**. Although dancers remember nothing of the communion that has taken place, *they are greatly* **empowered** *by the experience.*

Offerings and Sacrifice

As each spirit *MANIFESTS* itself, *it is greeted, honored, and presented with the appropriate* **offerings**. The ceremony culminates with **sacrifices** of the spirit's favorite animals, *which have been carefully reared and prepared.* The sacrifices are then *COOKED* for a **feast** at which the *SPIRITS* are the *GUESTS* of *HONOR*. It is hard for an uninitiated Westerner not to see Vodou as an amalgam of BARBARIC and ALARMING customs, *but there is something* **compelling** *and* **vivid** *about Vodou that* ATTRACTS *at the same time as it* REPELS *the* UNINITIATED.

Divine Messengers

In reality, Vodou is **spiritual** in a way that is UNMATCHED by the *abstracted, outer forms of the other major religions.* The LWA have much in common with the familiar anthropomorphic gods of the Greek and Germanic traditions. *They are archetypal ancestor spirits, both HUMAN and DIVINE.* The lesser *LWA* inhabit TREES, MOUNTAINS, CAVES, and STREAMS, just like the *NYMPHS*, *FAUNS*, and *DRYADS* of GREEK MYTHOLOGY. But this **pagan pantheism** operates beneath the COSMIC UNITY represented by BON DIEU, *the supreme creator god.* The *LWA* act as **divine messengers** mediating between HEAVEN and EARTH, *like* HERMES *in Greek mythology and the Hermetic tradition.* You do not have to have AFRICAN or ARAWAK blood, *or even be an adherent of Vodou,* in order to receive **possession**.

The Lwa

THE LWA EXIST ON AN INVISIBLE SPIRITUAL PLANE THAT MIRRORS THE MATERIAL WORLD. THEY ARE LIVING GODS WITH THE SAME IMPORTANT RESPONSIBILITIES THAT THE GODS HAVE ALWAYS HAD, SUCH AS THE WEATHER, LOVE, FERTILITY, DEATH, AND AGRICULTURE. THE LWA BELONG TO TWO PRINCIPAL CLANS, OR NANCHON: THE AFRICAN RADA AND THE HAITIAN PETWO, WHO SHARE SIMILAR ROLES BUT HAVE DIFFERENT OR OPPOSING PERSONALITIES.

The Rada Lwa

Listed below are some of the major lwa of the Rada nanchon.

PAPA LEGBA

As guardian of the crossroads, LEGBA is the **gatekeeper** between the two worlds. *Without his consent there can be no communication between* LWA *and* MORTALS. He is the **source** of all rituals. *He is represented as a* **cranky** *but* **lovable** *OLD MAN carrying a stick.* His colors are RED and WHITE, and his *OFFERINGS* include **grilled chicken**, **sweet potatoes**, and **tobacco**.

THE MARASA

After PAPA LEGBA, the first *LWA* to be honored in ceremonies are the **Divine Twins**, *who represent the duality of human existence—HALF HUMAN, HALF DIVINE*; HALF MORTAL, HALF IMMORTAL. The Marasa were the first humans, the first ancestors, and therefore the FIRST LWA. *They are the* **healers** *who prescribe herbal medicines during possession.* Their symbol is the **palm leaf**.

Ezili

The great goddess of Vodou is the ETERNAL FEMININE in all its complexity. As EZILI DANTÒ, *she is the dominating but homely matriarch*, identified with the **Black Madonna**. As EZILI FREDA, she is a PREENING, FLIRTING, LUXURY KITTEN, all *PINK CHAMPAGNE* and *FANCY CIGARETTES*, whose appearances are initially triumphant, but always end in tears. *She is the sacred* **bleeding heart**, whose love is defined by the SORROW it endures and to which there is no end as long as the worlds are divided. *As the* PETWO EZILI GE-ROUGE (*Red Eyes*), *her PAIN turns to* **fury**, *her SOBS to* **shrieks**, *and her LOVE to* **hatred**.

Danbala and Ayida Wèdo

The COSMIC COUPLE is represented by the **serpent** and the **rainbow**. DANBALA *is the cosmic serpent*, the creative life force of the universe, equated with **lightning** and **water**; AYIDA WÈDO *is his consort.* Together they give birth to the world and their symbol is an **egg**, which is also their principal offering.

Other Rada Lwa

Other important *RADA LWA* include AGWE and LASIREN, *the king and queen of the ocean*; PAPA ZAKA, *the god of agriculture*; OGOU, *a tribe of warrior spirits*; and LOKO ATISOU and AYIZAN, *patrons of the priesthood.*

Petwo—The Shadow Side

WHILE RADA REPRESENT THE SOCIAL AND HIERARCHICAL ASPECTS OF AN ORDERLY COSMOS, PETWO INCARNATE SUBVERSION AND DISORDER. THE GENTLER RADA SPIRITS SERVE THE COMMUNAL ASPECTS OF LIFE, WHILE THE PEPPERY, UNRELIABLE PETWO SPIRITS ARE PROPITIATED BY THOSE ON THE LEFT-HAND PATH, WHO SEARCH FOR PERSONAL POWER OR HAVE REVOLUTIONARY AGENDAS. WHERE RADA ARE SOMEWHAT DISTANT, PETWO ARE IMMEDIATE AND PRACTICAL. RADA DRUMMING IS ON THE BEAT AND RHYTHMIC, PETWO DRUMMING IS OFF-BEAT AND EDGY.

DON PETWO

Legend has it that PETWO worship was introduced by DON JEAN-PHILIPPE PEDRO in 1768. He is now revered as the father of the PETWO LWA, as DANBALA is to the RADA LWA. His son is a **serpent deity** (*like Danbala*) called TI-JEAN PETWO.

KALFU

While PAPA LEGBA is the SOLAR LORD of the CROSSROADS, *ruling the cardinal points*, KALFU is the **trickster** LUNAR LORD of the CROSSROADS, *ruling the points in between.* He rules the demons—the forces of disruption that can be controlled through sorcery. *His AMBIVALENCE is such that he can also protect people against sorcery.*

MARINETTE

Marinette is the principal female PETWO LWA, sometimes said to be the wife of TI-JEAN PETWO. She is POWERFUL, VIOLENT, and BLOODTHIRSTY, *like the Aztec corn goddess*, and capable, by her own admission, of the most appalling crimes. *Her familiar is an* **owl**.

Kriminel

KRIMINEL is one of the most demonic PETWO LWA and is summoned by the most ruthless **bòkòs** (*sorcerers*). *He is usually portrayed holding a* **knife** *in one hand and a* **severed head** *in the other.*

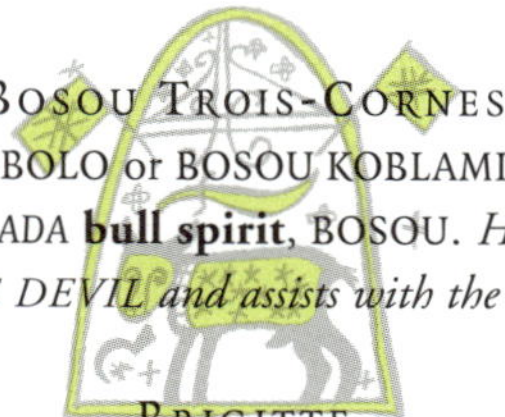

Bosou Trois-Cornes

Also known as DIOBOLO or BOSOU KOBLAMIN, this is a PETWO manifestation of the RADA **bull spirit**, BOSOU. *He is depicted as a little THREE-HORNED FIRE DEVIL and assists with the WORST kind of sorcery.*

Brigitte

Named after ST. BRIDGET, *Brigitte is the Guardian of Graves,* a powerful magical LWA of **cemeteries**. Her *SACRED TREES* are the **elm** and the **weeping willow**.

Papa Gede

The **Gede** group of LWA is neither RADA nor PETWO, though PAPA GEDE, *one of its two principal figures,* is often classified as RADA. PAPA GEDE is the **black sun**, *the fire in the darkness at the crossroads between life and death.* He is also the BAWDY, RIBALD JOKER, who delights in *LAMPOONING* those who are uncomfortable with their *SEXUALITY.*

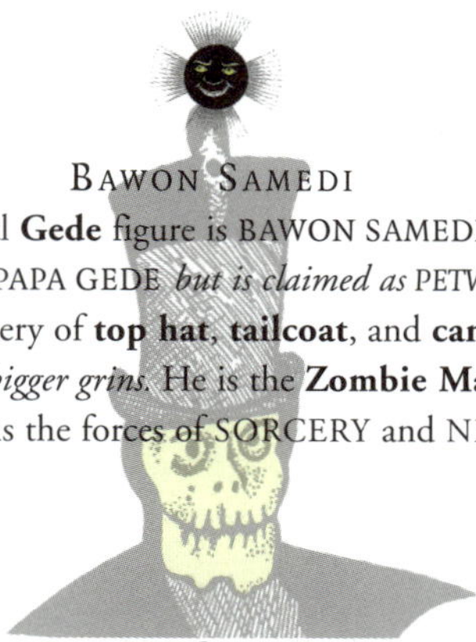

Bawon Samedi

The other principal **Gede** figure is BAWON SAMEDI, *who is almost interchangeable with* PAPA GEDE *but is claimed as* PETWO. He sports the **undertaker's** sinister finery of **top hat**, **tailcoat**, and **cane**, *set off with mirror shades, big cigars, and bigger grins.* He is the **Zombie Master**, LORD of the DEAD, who governs the forces of SORCERY and NECROMANCY.

Sorcery

The difference between RADA and PETWO is the difference between religion and magic. RELIGION *supports the role of essentially BENIGN DIVINE POWERS in maintaining the equilibrium of the world by REPLENISHING their ENERGIES through collective* WORSHIP. When **human beings** take divine power into their own hands to IMPROVE their POSITION, *it becomes magic.* The great RADA LWA cannot be persuaded to lend their authority to the ambitions of individuals. The more ambivalent PETWO LWA, such as KALFU and BAWON SAMEDI, on the other hand, will, **if correctly propitiated**, *allow access to occult power through the mediation of lesser* PETWO SPIRITS, such as KRIMINEL and BOSOU TROIS-CORNES. While the LWA can **confer power** on people, it is PEOPLE, not the LWA, who **perform** the magic.

SERVING WITH THE LEFT HAND

The Vodou **sorcerer** (BÒKÒ) is said to "*serve with the left hand*," while a high priest (OUNGAN) "*serves with the right hand*" or, possibly, both hands. *The* BÒKÒ *operates outside the natural law of the* RADA and is dependent on KALFU and BAWON SAMEDI, both for his access to power and his well-being, since the RADA LWA may **withhold** their **blessings** from sorcerers. Some BÒKÒS, particularly the **dreaded** VEAU-BÒKÒS, operate in groups, known as *RED SECTS*, that are much like *MASONIC BLACK LODGES.* *The* BÒKÒ *is usually willing to sell his services.* These include some of the most powerful sorcery techniques to be found in any culture.

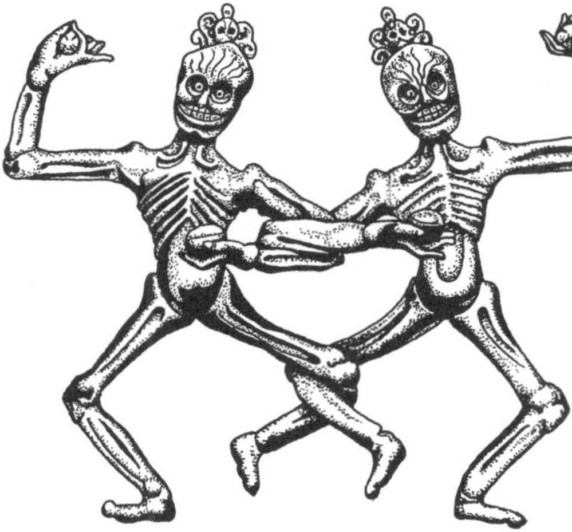

Zombies—The Walking Dead

The aspect of sorcery most peculiar to Vodou is the creation of **zombies**. *By STEALING somebody's soul, a BÒKÒ can render the body apparently LIFELESS.* The entombed "**corpse**" can be DISINTERRED and REANIMATED as a semi-conscious **automaton** to work as a slave. Some *BÒKÒS* use a powerful **poison** *extracted from the* **puffer fish** that PARALYZES certain neural centers in the BRAIN, *inducing a death-like catalepsy.* After being exhumed, the **terrified** and **brain-damaged** "zombie" is easily controlled.

Bakas

BAKAS are demonic entities that can be bound by powerful **talismans** known as WANGA. They can be directed to perform malevolent acts on behalf of a BÒKÒ *and assume ANIMAL FORM while about their business.* They are **dangerous** and **unpredictable** even in the hands of a powerful BÒKÒ *and can extract a high price for their services.* Other common forms of Vodou sorcery include *NECROMANCY* and the use of "**voodoo dolls**," effigies similar to those described on page 50.

Protection

Except in very RARE instances, *the only people who are at RISK from malevolent Vodou magic are those living in COMMUNITIES where it is PRACTICED*. Since the best way to counter any form of invasive magic is to **block the channels that it uses**, victims of VODOU MALPRACTICE should always seek out a reliable *OUNGAN* or *MANBO*, a **Vodou priest** or **priestess**, for expert help. *Here are some of the techniques most widely used.*

Paquets Kongo

These are protective **onion-shaped** talismanic charms containing various **herbs** and **powders** *that are carefully wrapped in cloth and adorned with a variety of BEADS, FEATHERS, SEQUINS, and RIBBONS* in colors corresponding to the *LWA* whose assistance is required. They are prepared during special FULL-MOON ceremonies under the auspices of SIMBI, *an important lwa of magic*, who is neither *RADA* nor *PETWO*. The **paquets** are tied with ribbon or string that has been *KNOTTED SEVEN TIMES* and retain their protective power for seven years.

Gardes

The OUNGAN and MANBO are also HEALERS. *In order to protect their people from the* **malevolent magic** *of the* BÒKÒ, they must sometimes PERFORM magic themselves. One of their magical functions is to provide GARDES as protection against the WANGA used by BÒKÒS. *These are done in the name of* KALFU, the LWA who controls **demons.** They may take the form of a TALISMAN, CHARM, SPELL (*also known as gri-gri*), or a MAGIC POTION *that is either* **drunk** *or* **rubbed** *into cuts in the* **skin**.

To petition a LWA for assistance, *Vodou believers often make little* **cloth dolls**, known as *MESSENGER DOLLS.* A **prayer** or **petition** is written on a piece of **paper** and TIED to the doll's WAIST with *STRING* or *RIBBON. The doll is then left in a* **cemetery** *or at a* **crossroads** *where the SPIRIT and HUMAN WORLDS meet.*

Magic Lamps

Oil lamps are used for several kinds of sympathetic magic and healing. *They usually consist of a* **small bowl of castor oil** *with added ingredients corresponding to one of the* LWA. More powerful lamps are sometimes used with more complex ingredients. A CRAB SHELL filled with *CASTOR OIL, CHILI PEPPERS, GRAVEYARD* or *CROSSROADS SOIL, RED PRECIPITATE,* and several other ingredients is used to ward off enemies or occult attack. *A* **bottle** *filled with similar ingredients also acts as a MAGIC LAMP to exorcise an evil spirit.* It **burns** for a week, after which it is CORKED, HUNG in the *OUNGAN* or *MANBO'S YARD*, and soundly **whipped** every day until it has achieved its purpose.

Chapter 6
VAMPIRISM

The word **vampire** is derived from the RUSSIAN verb **pi**, meaning "*to drain.*" A belief in vampires—*the dead who rise from the grave at night to suck the* **blood** *of the living*—is extremely ancient. It has been traced back to the ancient cultures of INDIA, GREECE, and BABYLON.

Vampires of the World

Although TRANSYLVANIA, in modern ROMANIA, *is the home of vampirism in Western legend and literature*, vampires are found all over the world. In certain *TRADITIONS* they are identified with **witches** or **werewolves**; *in others, they are not human but NOCTURNAL* **ghouls** *whose home is the spirit world.* In RUSSIA, UKRAINE, and MEXICO, they are sorcerers; in SERBIA and BULGARIA, the DECEASED can become vampires if ANIMALS JUMP or BIRDS FLY over their **corpses**.

VAMPIRE PLAGUES

Vampirism is by its very nature **epidemic**. When the victims of vampires die, *they become vampires themselves and go on to* **infect** *their own* **victims**. Eastern Europe, particularly the Slavic lands of HUNGARY, BOHEMIA, MORAVIA, and SILESIA, has been the scene of many bizarre and well-documented **vampire plagues**. In the 1730s there were several outbreaks with striking similarities: *a succession of unusual* **deaths**, *followed by the EXHUMATION of* **coffins** *that were found to contain large quantities of* **fresh blood** and the **lifeless** but **uncorrupted bodies** of people who could only be assumed to be vampires. The BEHEADING and BURNING of the corpses would end one plague, *but as soon as one* OUTBREAK *was QUELLED*, another broke out in a neighboring region.

Count Dracula—The Archetypal Vampire

The IRISH author BRAM STOKER created the world's most famous vampire, COUNT DRACULA, in 1897. Stoker combined elements from the **Gothic** vampire tales of DR POLIDORI and SHERIDAN LE FANU with historical allusions to VLAD DRACULA, *a sadistic, rather than vampiric, 15th-century prince of* WALACHIA (*in modern* ROMANIA), who earned the nickname "*Vlad the Impaler*" from the **gruesome** way he dealt with his enemies. Count Dracula is **irresistible**, *particularly to women,* because he is *SUAVE, SEDUCTIVE, MAGNETIC*, and *DEADLY*. The restless count has risen from his literary grave time and time again to star in hundreds of MOVIES, several STAGE PLAYS, and countless LITERARY SPIN-OFFS, *making him one of the best-known fictional characters in literary history.* His **immortality** is assured.

Vampire Lore

STOKER'S CLASSIC STORY IS RICH IN WELL-RESEARCHED HISTORICAL AND FOLKLORIC DETAIL, ESTABLISHING MANY OF THE KEY ASPECTS OF VAMPIRE LORE.

A vampire is immortal, but is quickened by *HUMAN BLOOD, ideally that of a VIRGIN.*

A vampire can be killed, but only in the following ways: *a WOODEN STAKE driven through the HEART*, a **silver bullet** through the heart or head, *exposure to sunlight or fire*, or *IMMERSION* in running water.

A vampire can be wounded by *HOLY WATER* or the sign of the *CROSS*.

Countess Bathory—Blood Ghoul

To the rational mind, *a MORBID FASCINATION for human blood in a living person is more understandable than a belief in the undead.* Just such a person—**a blood ghoul**—was the COUNTESS ELIZABETH BATHORY, whose forbear, PRINCE STEVEN BATHORY, had helped VLAD the IMPALER *regain his THRONE in 1476.*

The COUNTESS was born into one of the most *POWERFUL FAMILIES* of TRANSYLVANIA in 1560 *and was* **married** *to a military hero nicknamed the* BLACK KNIGHT *when she was 15.* When he died in 1600, she developed a **sadistic streak** and embarked on a **career of crime** with the help of her MANSERVANT and two *WITCHES. One day after a SERVANT GIRL'S blood got on her hand,* the Countess was convinced that her skin had been **rejuvenated**. She had the girl murdered and her blood drained into a bath in which the Countess then bathed. *Believing that she had discovered the* **elixir** *of eternal life and youth,* she went on a **killing spree** that was only checked when her taste for ARISTOCRATIC BLOOD led to complaints being made to the Emperor. When her castle was raided, *the* **bloodless corpse** *of a young woman was found in the hall and* **tortured girls** *in the cellars.* FIFTY BODIES were exhumed from beneath the castle walls. Her accomplices were tried for the crimes and executed, but the COUNTESS herself was **imprisoned in her castle** until her death in 1614.

Vampiric Spirits

Magical folklore around the world recounts tales of vampire spirits that feast on the blood of the living. One of the oldest examples is the ancient Greek myth of the lamia.

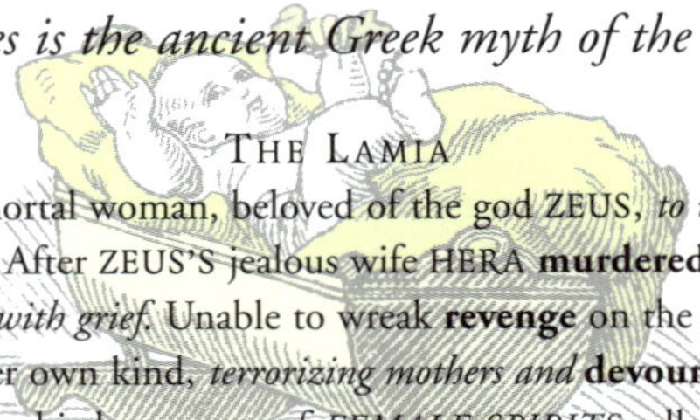

The Lamia

LAMIA was a mortal woman, beloved of the god ZEUS, *to whom she bore several children.* After ZEUS'S jealous wife HERA **murdered** her children, LAMIA *went mad with grief.* Unable to wreak **revenge** on the gods, she turned her **fury** on her own kind, *terrorizing mothers and* **devouring** *newborn children.* She gave birth to a race of *FEMALE SPIRITS* called **lamioi**, *who attach themselves to children in order to SUCK their BLOOD.* The ANCIENT GREEKS believed that any woman who **died in childbirth** might become a lamia. A similar belief exists in MEXICO, *where a bloodsucker spirit is known as a* **ciupipiltin**. In INDONESIA, these spirits are called **wewe**.

Incubi and Succubi

These demon spirits are as ancient as the LAMIOI and are referred to by SHAKESPEARE and many other classical writers. *An INCUBUS is a male spirit who has* **sexual intercourse** *with WOMEN while they are asleep,* while a SUCCUBUS is female spirit who does the same with men. Although they are not BLOODSUCKERS, *these spirits* **drain the energy** *of their mortal lovers and lead them into DAMNATION.* The *MALLEUS MALEFICARUM* (*15th-century witch-hunters' manual*) recommended that those found to have CONSORTED with such demon lovers should be **put to death**. Female VAMPIRE SPIRITS who **seduce** young men are known as **puntianak** in MALAYSIA and INDONESIA.

Psychic Vampirism

Many of us have had the experience of feeling **strangely drained** *after we have been with certain people.* However, the INDIVIDUALS concerned might not be aware of the effect they are having. Others, including STAGE PERFORMERS, HYPNOTISTS, and CHARISMATIC LEADERS, are adept at **captivating** the attention of their audience, *but in this case the process is RECIPROCAL and there is no loss of energy.* There are occult techniques, however, for **sucking** out the **vitality** of a living person just as a VAMPIRE SUCKS out BLOOD. *Some occultists use* **astral projection** *to visit their victims WHILE THEY SLEEP and drain them of their vital energy.* They may deliberately awaken them in order to terrify them, **or they may work in secret**, *making it very difficult for their victims to* **diagnose** *or* **confront** *the cause of their* **suffering**.

This *PHENOMENON* is becoming more widely recognized and ties in with the **folklore** about vampire sorcerers, such as the MEXICAN NAHUALLI. A related and relatively *COMMON PHENOMENON* is that of the "*night hag,*" which is when people wake up **paralyzed** *with a crushing weight on their* **chests** *and a terrible sense of* **dread**. The night hag may be a ghost or demon, *but it could also be an* **occult attack** *by a SORCERER.*

Defense Techniques

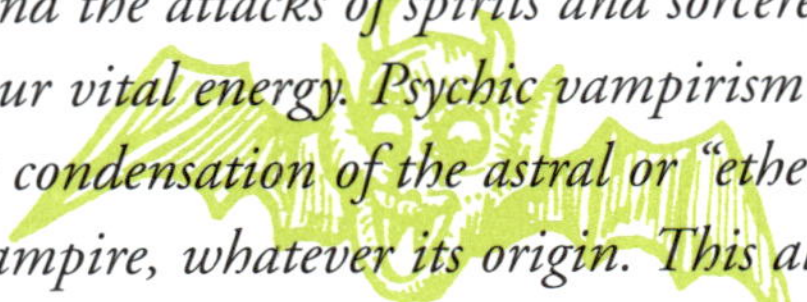

There are various defenses that will protect you from vampires, and the attacks of spirits and sorcerers who seek to drain your vital energy. Psychic vampirism takes place through the condensation of the astral or "etheric" energies of the vampire, whatever its origin. This allows the vampire direct access to your own etheric body, which it can then tap. Fortunately there are several ways of preventing this from happening.

GARLIC

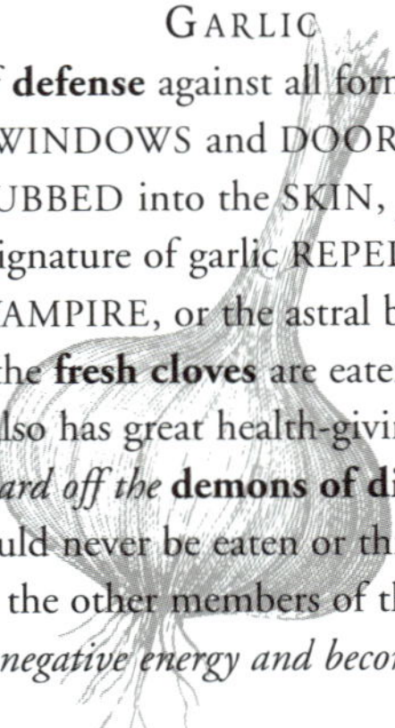

The classic first line of **defense** against all forms of vampirism is GARLIC. This can be **hung** in WINDOWS and DOORWAYS or, *in extremis*, **fresh garlic juice** can be RUBBED into the SKIN, *particularly on the neck and wrists.* The vibrational signature of garlic REPELS all kinds of spirits, be they ANGEL, DEMON, VAMPIRE, or the astral body of a SORCERER. It is particularly effective if the **fresh cloves** are eaten, *as it then PERMEATES the entire body.* The **bulb** also has great health-giving benefits. *It has* **antibiotic properties** *and can ward off the* **demons of disease**. Garlic that has been hung in a room should never be eaten or thrown away; *IT MUST BE BURNED*. Like the other members of the ONION FAMILY, *it absorbs negative energy and becomes* **poisonous**.

CRYSTALS

AMETHYST and AVENTURINE crystals can stop psychic vampires from entering any room in which they are placed. *Since amethyst is relatively INEXPENSIVE and readily available*, it makes an ideal protective amulet that can be set in **silver** *and worn around the* **neck**.

Vinegar

Another effective method to protect yourself from vampires and other occult attacks is to **dissolve consecrated salt** (*see the recipe for holy water on pages 186–187*) in **vinegar** and pour it into **saucers** *that you should then place around your BEDROOM.*

Water and Salt

Vampires operate on both the psychic and material planes, *which are represented by the elements WATER and EARTH.* These two elements are in turn represented by WATER and SALT. Salt, **being crystalline**, *is easy to charge with psychic energy*, as is fresh water. This is why HOLY WATER (*which contains salt*) is used for both **baptisms** and **exorcisms**. *Water is purifying because it absorbs and dissolves ETHERIC ENERGY.* This explains why vampires cannot CROSS running water—*it literally SUCKS their substance away.* Taking a **bath** to which you have added a few drops of HOLY WATER is an excellent way to purify your **aura**. If you follow this by wearing FRESH NIGHTCLOTHES, *moving your bed so that you sleep facing a DIFFERENT DIRECTION*, and sleeping in fresh sheets, you will effectively MASK YOUR PRESENCE from any **marauding vampire**.

Chapter 7
Haunting

A **ghost** is the *RESTLESS SPIRIT* of a DECEASED PERSON who haunts the abodes of the living, unable or unwilling to accept the *FUTILITY* of its **discarnate half-life**. Ghosts are capable of various kinds of haunting, including making "*things go bump in the night.*"

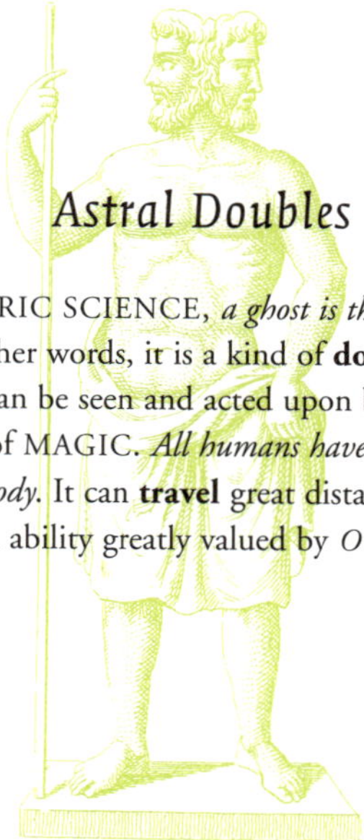

Astral Doubles

According to ESOTERIC SCIENCE, *a ghost is the spirit or astral body of a human being.* In other words, it is a kind of **double** that exists on the ASTRAL PLANE and can be seen and acted upon by CLAIRVOYANTS and PRACTITIONERS of MAGIC. *All humans have an astral double that is linked to their physical body.* It can **travel** great distances during **astral flight**, which is an ability greatly valued by *OCCULTISTS.*

Other Types of Spirits

There are other spirits that are also capable of doing hauntings, *including* **poltergeists** *and various tribes of the FAIRY RACE*, the so-called "*little people.*" It is not always easy to DETERMINE what kind of spirit is RESPONSIBLE for a haunting, *so we shall look at the most likely suspects in turn.*

Ghosts

All cultures believe in an **afterlife**—*that an essential, but immaterial, part of us SURVIVES physical* **death** *and moves on to another stage of existence,* be it some kind of HEAVEN, HELL, UNDERWORLD, or REINCARNATION. The ANCIENT EGYPTIANS, who had a profound understanding of all aspects of death, taught that the *IMMORTAL SOUL* (*ba*) separated from the body and astral spirit (*ka*) at the moment of death and **flew to heaven**, after which it might **reincarnate**.

The KA would seek to SUSTAIN *its* IDENTITY *until it was ready to dissipate.* **Tombs** would be filled with all the things the *KA* needed to facilitate its PEACEFUL PASSING. If not sufficiently provided for, *the KA might leave the tomb and* **haunt** *its friends and relatives to provide it with* **etheric sustenance** *in the form of PSYCHIC or EMOTIONAL ENERGY*—in the same way as a PSYCHIC VAMPIRE.

Astral Nourishment

The astral body is the instrument of PASSIONS, EMOTIONS, and DESIRES. It retains this function even after death when it is **separated** from the physical body, *of which it is an EXACT image.* Those that have died a *VIOLENT, TORTURED*, or *SUDDEN DEATH* are charged with shock or emotion, *giving them a* **temporarily enhanced vitality** *that they can SUSTAIN INDEFINITELY by* **refueling** *their* **energies** *by absorbing the emotional energies of the living.* A ghost may not even know that it is dead, in which case it will continue its habitual existence, *PUZZLED and increasingly FRETFUL that it is being IGNORED by the living.* **Anger** is a powerfully PROJECTED EMOTION that can allow a ghost to become visible even to those normally INSENSITIVE to the astral plane.

The **fear** that its appearance inevitably induces is readily **absorbed** by the ghost, *making it aware that such tactics provide a useful source of ASTRAL NOURISHMENT.* Like a SERIAL KILLER or VAMPIRE, a ghost can become OBSESSED with **preying** on the living to **sustain** its identity. This ability to absorb energy accounts for the common experience of people feeling **cold** and **depressed** in haunted places or prior to the appearance of a ghost. *These symptoms CEASE within a short time after the affected person LEAVES the LOCALE of the haunting.*

Black Spots

Occasionally hauntings are known to cause accident "**black spots**." *This can happen when the ghost of a* **road-accident victim** *LINGERS at the location of its death.* It seems that the ghosts of some accident victims may get caught in a kind of PSYCHIC LOOP, *endlessly REPEATING the circumstances of their DEATH.*

The following story is a typical example of such an accident "**black spot**." A couple driving along a **winding country road** were greatly ALARMED to be overtaken on a **blind bend** by a white PORSCHE driving at dangerously high speed. *A moment later the EXACT SAME THING happened again.* When they described the incident to the person they were visiting, *they were* **shocked** *to learn that a young man driving a white Porsche had died in a* **fatal accident** *on the very same road a week earlier.* The couple had had a LUCKY ESCAPE. Had the PORSCHE been coming toward them on the wrong side of the road, they might have SWERVED to avoid the **phantom car** and had a **serious accident** themselves.

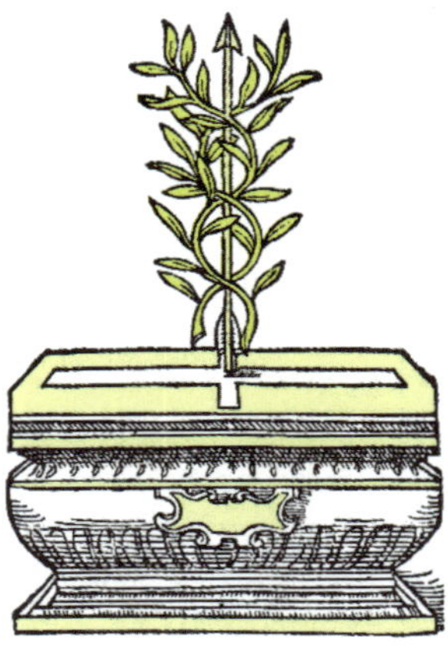

Poltergeists

Poltergeist means "*rattling ghost,*" but many of them do much more than rattle. They **throw** objects around rooms, **break** WINDOWS, **smash** DISHES, **interfere** with ELECTRICITY, *and even start fires.* The RUSSIAN parapsychologist ALEXANDER AKSAKOF recorded an instance where a *BLUISH PHOSPHORESCENT SPARK* **flew** through the air and **ignited** a woman's cotton dress. *The woman's husband was badly* **burned** *when he put out the fire but she was UNHARMED.*

Poltergeists are RARE but ANCIENT phenomena. *Their activities have been recorded all over the world for at least 3,000 years.* Some of these MALEVOLENT SPIRITS can communicate by **rapping** or even by **writing**. During a famous poltergeist haunting at AMHERST, NOVA SCOTIA, an **invisible hand** wrote in **fresh plaster**: "*Esther Cox, you are mine to kill.*"

Demonic or Mischievous?

Poltergeist activity is most frequent in the vicinity of particular types of people: CHILDREN, YOUNG WOMEN, those with EPILEPSY, *or persons suffering from mental disorders*; **prepubescent girls** are among the most common *MEDIUMS* for *POLTERGEISTS.* Certain poltergeists choose their victims, whom they follow from house to house, *while others stay in the same house and FRIGHTEN whoever is living there.* It is not certain what kind of spirit a POLTERGEIST is. Some authorities believe that they are GHOSTS, others that they are LESSER DEMONS, while in EUROPE they were once thought to be **mischievous house elves** like **goblins** or **kobolds**. A more recent theory is that they are physical manifestations of the unconscious human mind caused by **telekinesis**—*the ability to MOVE objects by THOUGHT alone.*

The Little People

All the fairy tribes—like ghosts—are spirits that exist on the astral plane. Many are nature spirits, like elementals and flower fairies, that are entirely preoccupied with their particular tasks of overseeing natural phenomena; others are more akin to lesser angelic or demonic entities.

House Spirits

Some of the FAIRY FOLK are fascinated by human activity and choose to live in CLOSE PROXIMITY to us, *dwelling in our HOMES, SHOPS, OFFICES, and FACTORIES*. In the GERMANIC tradition, **kobolds** were originally SUBTERRANEAN SPIRITS presiding over **mineral activity**, just like the CORNISH "*knockers.*" Disturbed by the intrusion of **miners**, some assisted the miners in their activities, *while others proved to be deadly, causing* **cave-ins** *and* **explosions**. Others followed the INVADERS up to the surface, intrigued as to what the miners intended to do with the metals and minerals they had mined. *Those that found our homes AGREEABLE and were attracted to their WARMTH invited themselves in as* **lodgers**. The term HOBGOBLIN refers to a kind of HOUSE ELF that likes to haunt the **hob**, *an old word for hearth.*

GUARDIANS AND TRICKSTERS

Our relationship with house elves has not always been HARMONIOUS. Opinions about them vary widely. *They might be* FRIENDLY, USEFUL, MISCHIEVOUS, *or MALEVOLENT SPAWNS of the DEVIL.* **Brownies** and the ANDEAN **ekkeko** have the reputation of being **shy**, but **helpful** around the house. HOBGOBLINS and KOBOLDS are considered **childish** and **mischievous**, *but HARMLESS and even USEFUL if well treated.* **Goblins**, on the other hand, have a reputation for MALICIOUSNESS. They are said to **delight** in any **discord** they can provoke.

It is malicious or tricky fairy spirits that are capable of POLTERGEIST activity. Among the SLAVIC peoples of RUSSIA and EASTERN EUROPE, house elves are known as **domovoi**, *and are considered useful guardians.* If treated with respect, DOMOVOI are said to be very **loyal**, following their human family wherever they move. They are *EASILY ANGERED*, however, *whereupon they might perform many of the UPSETTING TRICKS associated with poltergeists.* In SLAVIC countries, poltergeist activity has traditionally always been blamed on **disgruntled domovoi**.

Pest Control

There is a RICH FOLK TRADITION about how to **evict** troublesome spirits. *Different methods are prescribed for different types of spirits.* Some of these methods come under the term "*to lay*," meaning to **settle** or **calm**. We still talk of "*laying a ghost to rest*," though usually as a METAPHOR.

Exorcism

In the case of ghosts and demonic spirits, the standard procedure is exorcism, *which is dealt with in some detail on pages 178–187.* Certain ghosts simply need to be RECOGNIZED and UNDERSTOOD. *In such cases, a SENSITIVE, SYMPATHETIC, FEARLESS PERSON may be able to lay a ghost by* **connecting** *with it and* **reassuring** *it sufficiently to render it harmless or even* **encourage** *it to DISSOLVE.* In other cases, particularly when dealing with demonic entities, only exorcism is likely to succeed in laying or removing the TROUBLESOME SPIRIT. Exorcism requires the services of a TRAINED EXORCIST and should **not** be *ATTEMPTED* by the *UNINITIATED.*

Placating Fairy Spirits

LAYING A FAIRY USUALLY IMPLIES GETTING RID OF IT, BUT IT IS WORTH TRYING THE FOLLOWING METHODS TO PLACATE A SPIRIT THAT MAY BE TROUBLING YOU.

- **Be careful not to refer to any fairy spirits directly**. Never use the term BROWNIE, ELF, or HOBGOBLIN openly in the house. This is why **euphemisms** such as the "*little people*," "*good folk*," or "*good fellows*" are used.

- **Leave a little food out**, such as MILK and BISCUITS. *Fairies can absorb the ETHERIC ENERGY available in food,* so **don't** EAT what they leave behind.

Laying a Fairy

THERE ARE SEVERAL WELL-KNOWN METHODS FOR LAYING PROBLEMATIC HOUSE ELVES THAT, IF THEY WORK AT ALL, MAY WORK ON THOSE POLTERGEISTS THAT ARE WICKED OR DISGRUNTLED SPRITES.

- **Laying out little suits of clothing** while saying out loud that they are intended as a **gift** to the LITTLE PEOPLE is considered a **foolproof** way of laying house elves, *although exactly why is uncertain*. One tradition says that it **offends** them, while another claims that it makes them **too proud** to associate with humans.

- **Scattering seeds**, particularly tiny seeds like POPPY, *on the ground is said to distract sprites from causing mischief.* They feel *COMPELLED* to *GATHER UP* all the seed and have no time for mischief, or else they become **exasperated** and leave of their own accord.

- **Sprinkling salt** around the home, *particularly in the corners*, can help lay a fairy. Like VAMPIRES, they are said to **hate** SALT.

- **Placing a sock under the bed** is a BAFFLING but WELL-ATTESTED WAY to discourage *DISRUPTIVE SPIRITS.*

- **Although poltergeists like to make a racket**, most spirits hate LOUD NOISES because the VIBRATIONS upset them. SHOUTING, CLAPPING, and BANGING **pots** and **pans** is an effective way to get rid of them.

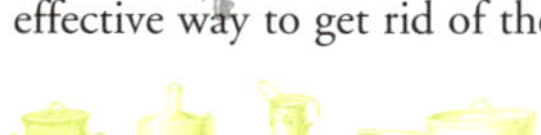

Chapter 8
POSSESSION

There are **many** DIFFERENT WAYS in which a spirit can **possess** a human being. Strictly speaking, *possession involves an ALTERED STATE of CONSCIOUSNESS in which the personality of an individual is replaced by that of another*—from an **occult** point of view, the CONSCIOUSNESS of ANOTHER ENTITY such as a **spirit** or **demon**.

Voluntary and Involuntary Possession

Vodou is a **possession religion**. *In Vodou, however, ritual possession is welcomed.* MEDIUMS and CHANNELERS invite **temporary possession** to **communicate** with the spirits and the gods. Involuntary possession, however, is usually much less welcome. *There are various kinds of possession.* Some, such as DEMONIC POSSESSION, exhibit unmistakable and **terrifying symptoms**, *while others can be much more insidious and hard to spot.* Various kinds of spirits may be involved, including DEMONS, GHOSTS, INCUBI, SUCCUBI, DISEASE SPIRITS, and IMPS or ELEMENTALS directed by **sorcerers**, such as the *DEVILISH BAKAS* of Vodou sorcerers.

Demonic Possession

Although many humans are the **unwitting hosts** of negative spirits of one kind or another, *one of the most TERRIBLE things that can happen to anybody is to be the VICTIM of DEMONIC POSSESSION.* Such forms of possession can have the most APPALLING CONSEQUENCES for the victims and their loved ones. One of the things that made the **novel** and **movie** *THE EXORCIST* so effective was that it was based on a very **real understanding of the dynamics** of demonic possession. Its *INSIGHT* was drawn principally from the *SCHOLARLY* work of T.K. OESTERREICH.

Historical Cases

There have been many FAMOUS and WELL-DOCUMENTED cases of demonic possession. **Three** of the best known occurred in 17TH-CENTURY FRANCE. *In each case a* **nun** *exhibited signs of demonic possession that proved CONTAGIOUS by INFECTING other nuns in the* **convent**. INVESTIGATIONS and EXORCISMS followed, resulting in **priests** being accused of **sorcery**, **diabolism**, and **fornication**. *In all three cases the accused priests were found* **guilty** *and BURNED ALIVE.*

THE DEVILS OF LOUDUN

Perhaps the most **famous** of the three cases involved a **charismatic priest** named URBAIN GRANDIER, *who was alleged to have made a PACT with the DEVIL* **sealed** *with his own BLOOD*. The document is preserved in the BIBLIOTHÈQUE NATIONALE in PARIS. Although there is good evidence that GRANDIER was **falsely accused by jealous rivals**, *the possession of the NUNS was very real and actually got worse after GRANDIER'S execution.* Almost every nun in the URSULINE CONVENT of LOUDUN was infected and showed all the signs of demonic possession. The affected nuns **talked in tongues**, engaged in **lewd behavior**, and spoke in **diabolical voices** claiming to be the **archdemons** ASMODEUS, LEVIATHAN, BALAM, and BEHEMOTH. *Repeated attempts at EXORCISM failed until the HEROIC PERSISTENCE of the* **saintly** PÈRE SURIN *finally succeeded in freeing the victims.*

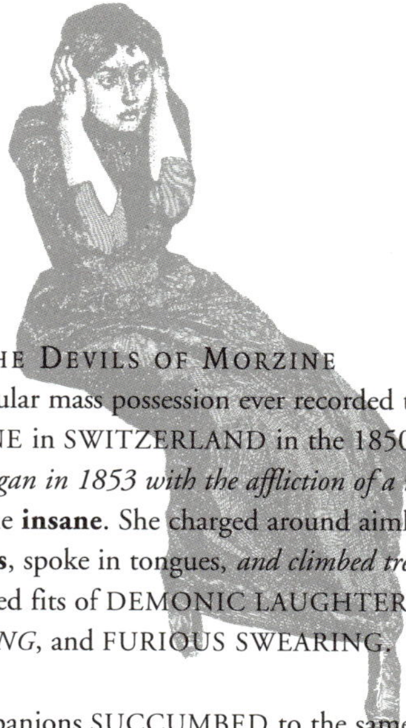

The Devils of Morzine

Perhaps the most spectacular mass possession ever recorded took place in the small village of MORZINE in SWITZERLAND in the 1850s, **and infected over 2,000 people**. *It began in 1853 with the affliction of a modest young girl,* who appeared to have gone **insane**. She charged around aimlessly, **writhed in agony**, imitated **animals**, spoke in tongues, *and climbed trees and buildings like a squirrel.* She suffered fits of DEMONIC LAUGHTER, *HYSTERICAL WEEPING*, and FURIOUS SWEARING.

Several of her companions SUCCUMBED to the same madness, *and within 20 days some 50 women and girls were similarly afflicted.* Soon it had become an **epidemic** of such EXTREME PROPORTIONS that the FRENCH EMPEROR LOUIS-NAPOLÉON sent three companies of **soldiers** to quell the disturbance. When this made matters worse an **army of priests** was sent but again to no avail. *The madness eventually petered out as quickly as it had started and was dismissed by MEN of SCIENCE as a case of* **mass hysteria**. Exactly how such hysteria could have seized the modest inhabitants of a quiet Swiss village has never been RATIONALLY EXPLAINED.

Other Types of Possession

Most types of possession MANIFEST in much LESS OBVIOUS ways than demonic possession. Spirits operating on the **astral plane** find it relatively easy to attach themselves to living people without their knowledge, particularly WEAK-WILLED or HYPERSENSITIVE INDIVIDUALS. Instant acute possession is **rare**, however. *It usually takes such spirits quite a long time to gain a high degree of control over their* **hosts**. Signs to look out for are MANIC DEPRESSION, HEARING VOICES, SUBSTANCE DEPENDENCE, particularly **alcoholism**, and COMPULSIVE BEHAVIOR, often of a **sexual nature**.

Parasites

The presence of parasitic spirits often manifests on the material plane as an **infestation** of *INTESTINAL* or *TISSUE* **parasites**. These can cause all kinds of systemic problems that MIRROR an increasing degree of CONTROL assumed by spirit parasites.

Disease Demons

The ancient, almost UNIVERSAL, belief in disease demons is first found in the demonology of ANCIENT BABYLONIA, a cradle of the Dark Arts, where they were referred to as "*the beloved sons of* BEL" (BEL *was a Babylonian deity*). These **parasitic spirits**, which may be inflicted on a person by sorcery, are likely to choose such insidious parasites as **nematodes** and **flukes** as their material manifestation. FLUKES *can carry* **viruses** *in the body for years.* They affect many people and are very **hard to get rid of**. *An effective method for getting rid of all parasites is provided on pages 129–130.*

Self-protection

The first line of **defense** against infestation by parasitic spirits is a STRONG WILL. This can be *DEVELOPED* through many of the techniques described in PART TWO of this book. *Strong-willed people have powerful* **auras** *that act as* **shields** *around them and can REPEL all but the most determined and powerfully directed ASTRAL ENTITIES.* The techniques available to you for building a strong aura involve FOCUS, CLARITY, and SELF-DISCIPLINE. These in turn help build **willpower** and **strength of character**.

Breaking Debilitating Habits

Many ghosts stay in **limbo** because of the **addictions** and **cravings** they nurtured while alive. *They will seek out people with similar addictions in order to feed their habits.* By LATCHING onto an *ADDICT* or an *ALCOHOLIC*, they can experience the **associated sensations** that they crave. *SEXUAL PERVERSION* and *OBSESSION* are other spiritual afflictions that keep ghosts trapped on the ASTRAL PLANE. A powerful ghost will be able to lead a **susceptible host** in any direction it chooses. *By breaking NEGATIVE HABITS, OBSESSIONS, and ADDICTIONS, we deprive such spirits of the experiences they* **crave** *and make ourselves* **unsuitable hosts**.

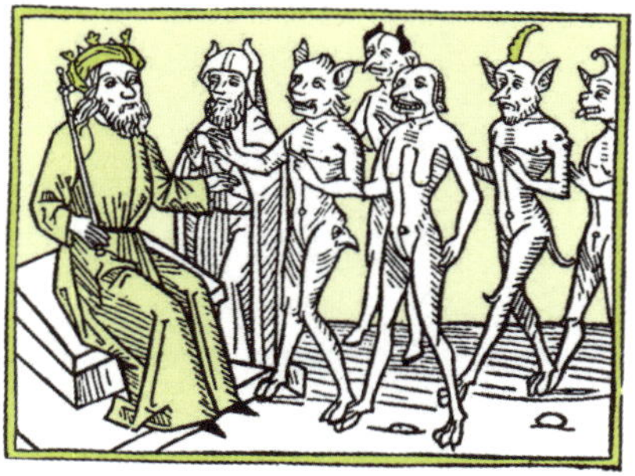

Exorcism

There are many ways to prevent possession, *but once a parasitic spirit has gained a high level of control over its host,* there is only *ONE CURE*: **exorcism**. Exorcism involves the **expulsion** of UNWELCOME SPIRITS from a person or place by means of PRAYERS, COMMANDS, and RELIGIOUS RITUALS. The ancient Jewish historian JOSEPHUS tells us that KING SOLOMON had been taught this "*useful and sanative*" art by GOD. He writes that SOLOMON, "*left behind him the manner of using exorcisms, by which they drive away demons, so that they never return. And this method of cure is of great force unto this day.*" Exorcism has been a standard part of **Christian practice** since at least the 3rd century A.D.

To deal effectively with powerful possessing spirits requires a profound *UNDERSTANDING* of *DEMONOLOGY* and also enormous STRENGTH of FAITH on the part of the **exorcist**, *whether he or she is an ordained priest or not.* The presence of an exorcist can drive a possessed person into a **violent frenzy**, creating a DANGEROUS SITUATION for all present, particularly the exorcist, *who may become possessed by the very spirit he or she seeks to exorcise.* Exorcists do not, of course, have to be CHRISTIAN, and **equivalent rituals and techniques** are used in other faiths and traditions.
Exorcism is described in detail on pages 178–187.

Part Two

Self-defense

All human beings encounter difficulties in their lives: ILLNESS, DEPRESSION, ACCIDENTS, and other kinds of MISFORTUNE. In rare cases, this could be due to an occult attack by demons and ghosts that have been sent to PLAGUE you by a sorcerer. To PROTECT YOURSELF from bad luck and evil influences, you can use a variety of magical techniques to build a shield of protection, such TALISMANS, AMULETS, MANTRAS, and ANGEL MAGIC.

Chapter 1

Symptoms and Diagnosis

If you think you may be the VICTIM of **occult attack**, the first thing you should do is ANALYZE your *SYMPTOMS* and *LIFESTYLE*. However, keep in mind that occult attack is the **least likely** reason for your symptoms. Always look for NONMAGICAL causes and *deal with them appropriately*, **seeking help** from a qualified DOCTOR if necessary.

Self-analysis

Most forms of OCCULT INTERFERENCE that affect humans are caused by **parasitic spirits**. Some of these can be directed by sorcery, *but many are the astral shells of dead humans—GHOSTS*—who do not require the aid of a practitioner of the Dark Arts to find their victims. To find a **cure**, you need to look at the wider picture: *LIFESTYLE, PAST HISTORY, CONTACTS, WEAKNESSES*, and other contributing factors. The first thing to do, however, as in any medical situation, is to **analyze the symptoms**. Below is a list of possible symptoms, *but remember that they are far more likely to be medical rather than magical problems*, and should be dealt with accordingly.

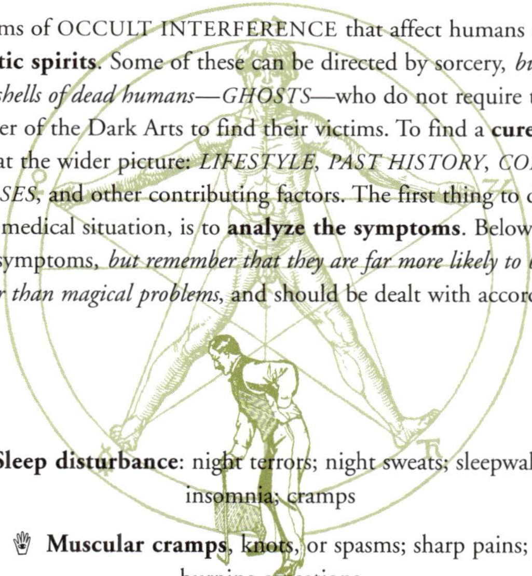

- **Sleep disturbance**: night terrors; night sweats; sleepwalking; insomnia; cramps
- **Muscular cramps**, knots, or spasms; sharp pains; burning sensations
- **Autoimmune problems**: arthritis; hepatitis; psoriasis; Crohn's disease; diabetes
- **Immune system problems**: allergies; asthma; skin conditions; sinus problems
- **Stomach and bowel problems**; dietary intolerances
- **Neurological and mood disorders**: depression; mood swings; anger; anxiety; confusion; mania; neurosis
- **Obsessive-compulsive behavior patterns**; erratic behavior; sexual perversion
- **A series of misfortunes**, calamities, or accidents

SLEEP DISTURBANCES

The **subconscious mind** is the first part of the self to detect occult interference, *which is why one of the INITIAL SIGNS of an attack is sleep disturbance.* **Night terrors** are much less common than nightmares. Unlike nightmares, they involve no REM activity, which indicates that they do not share the same mechanism. *Terrors can induce* NIGHT SWEATS, CRAMPS, *and temporary* PARALYSIS. A typical form of night attack exerts CRUSHING PRESSURE on the chest, an acute SENSE of DREAD, and an INABILITY to MOVE. The best way to free yourself is to summon up all your willpower and **cry out** as loudly as possible. Such attacks can induce **anxious insomnia**—*either an inability to sleep or a fear of sleep.*

CRAMPS AND PAINS

Parasitic spirits can attach themselves to the **astral bodies** of the living. Their presence can be felt in the physical body (*of which the astral is an invisible double*) as knots of tension, causing STIFFNESS, MUSCULAR CRAMPS, and SPASMS. *These can be relieved by MASSAGE, ACUPUNCTURE, and gentle EXERCISE,* but they are always liable to return until the **parasite** has been **expelled** for good.

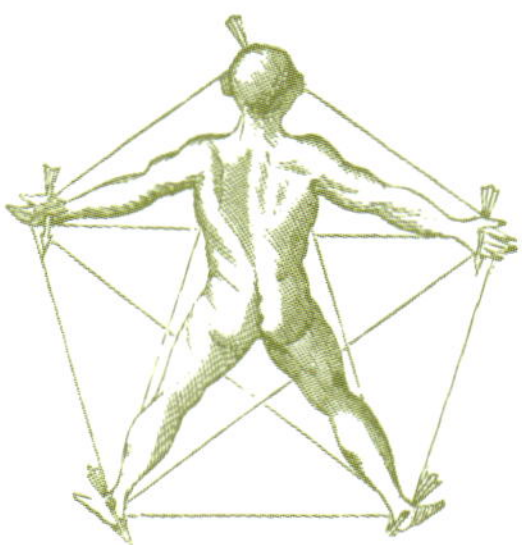

Physical Ill-health

By **weakening** the body's defense systems, parasitic spirits can take a firmer grip and exercise greater control. *Their presence can give rise to all kinds of physical problems*, particularly those involving the **immune system**. The body can develop new ALLERGIES, ASTHMA, and SKIN CONDITIONS, and **autoimmune problems** like *DIABETES* and *CHRONIC FATIGUE SYNDROME. Stomach disorders and dietary problems are also signs of weakened resistance and often require a complete change of lifestyle to combat them effectively.* **Pharmaceutical drugs** can effectively RELIEVE the symptoms of some of these conditions, but they cannot stop a **negative entity** from ATTACKING the HOST in a different part of his or her body.

Infirmities of the Spirit

Parasitic entities are, to quote an old-fashioned expression, "*highly vexatious to the spirit.*" They can inspire their hosts to generate bursts of **emotional energy** through VIOLENT MOOD SWINGS, OBSESSIVE MANIAS, and PERVERSE ACTIVITIES. They feed on this energy while their hosts become increasingly *DEPRESSED*, *NEUROTIC*, and *CONFUSED. A sovereign cure for all these disorders is the humble herb ST. JOHN'S WORT.* Long considered a SACRED AMULET against evil, it is now even recognized **pharmacologically** as a very useful remedy for **neurological problems**. It can rally the whole of one's being to *RESIST* all manner of evil. *It is widely available in pharmacies and health food stores*, but it is wise to consult an herbal physician before embarking on SELF-TREATMENT.

Likely Targets

Anyone can become the victim of a psychic attack, *but parasitic entities tend to choose EASY TARGETS*. **Strong characters** with POWERFUL WILLS, *and* POSITIVE, CONFIDENT *people tend to have powerful auras and strong psychic defenses*, regardless of their spiritual awareness. Naturally, the spirits will avoid them and attack more *SUSCEPTIBLE* people. These include people who are **sensitive** to PSYCHIC DISTURBANCES; people with **addictions**, particularly DRINKERS; **impressionable** people with low **self-esteem**; and people of an **anxious** or **nervous** disposition.

Lifestyle

The way we live our lives has an enormous bearing on our physical and spiritual well-being. There are certain lifestyle factors that can damage our defensive shield and increase the risk of attack. These include the following.

Hallucinogenic Drugs

Certain **psychoactive** drugs can increase our sensitivity to occult energies. **Hallucinogenic** drugs like LSD can generate both *HEAVENLY* and *HELLISH* experiences, *depending on factors such as mind-set and setting.* A bad trip can make people **hypersensitive** to negative energies and highly vulnerable to attack. The effects of the drug can amplify negative emotions like FEAR and ANXIETY in a way that shouts "*come and get me*" to any passing parasitic spirit. An experienced **shamanic healer** can employ sacred drugs like **peyote** and **ayahuasca** to strengthen the body's defensive shields, and can even get rid of SPIRITUAL LEECHES with the help of such drugs, but experimentation without an EXPERIENCED GUIDE is a very **risky** business.

Addiction

When you die, your ASTRAL SHELL continues to experience the same **cravings** and **obsessions** that you had when you were alive. *It is the desire to FEED these cravings that keeps many ghosts EARTHBOUND and attracts them to living people with the same addictions as themselves.* Being an addict—**to drugs, drink, or sex**—makes you an immediate target. It also tends to WEAKEN your SHIELD, making you more vulnerable to other forms of occult interference and psychic attack. This is why BUDDHISM and other spiritual paths encourage **abstinence** and **nonattachment**.

Alcohol and Tobacco

More people are addicted to alcohol and tobacco than to any other substances. **Tobacco addiction**, *while DETRIMENTAL to physical health*, has a much less pronounced effect on the spirit. It is primarily a **physical** addiction and tends to die with us rather than being passed on as a **craving** to the astral shell. **Alcoholism**, on the other hand, *is a much more complex addiction*, which tends to exaggerate negative tendencies. The change in personality so typical in alcoholics can be an indication of negative spirits taking over. *The ghosts of alcoholics have* **powerful cravings** *and seek out living alcoholics as* **hosts**.

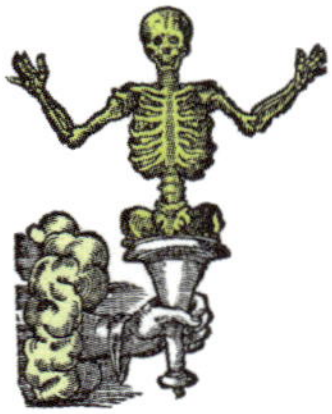

Dabbling in the Occult

Satanists may not represent as great a THREAT to society as people sometimes fear, but exposure to satanic rites can INFECT unsuspecting **thrill seekers** with all kinds of *NEGATIVE INFLUENCES* that can then infect others. The BLACK EUCHARIST often contains the **excrement** and **semen** of powerful negative people. *Eating it can create strong links with them that can be used as CHANNELS for occult interference.* Contact with people with such high exposure levels can be **dangerous**.

Any kind of OCCULT activity that involves INVITING SPIRITS to *COMMUNICATE* with you or through you is dangerous, *even if it is only a game.* **Ouija boards** and any kind of **séance** involving inexperienced mediums are particularly risky and often expose *INQUISITIVE, EXCITABLE young people to negative spiritual influences.*

Chapter 2

The Auric Shield

A subtle **energy field** known as an aura SURROUNDS everything in NATURE. Visible to the **psychically inclined** and, *under certain conditions*, to ordinary humans, the aura is depicted as a HALO or CORONA of FIERY LIGHT in religious iconography. The health of your aura is **crucial** to your WELL-BEING.

Composition of the Aura

The aura consists of a number of different **layers** or **levels**, *the inner ones of which correspond to your* EMOTIONAL, MENTAL, PHYSICAL, *and* SPIRITUAL SELVES. The aura is in a *CONSTANT* state of *FLUX*, changing with your **actions** and **emotions**. Its size depends on many different factors. *A healthy aura extends 4–10 feet (1–3 meters) in every direction.* It affects and is affected by your PHYSICAL HEALTH, your SPIRITUAL WELL-BEING, and everything you do. *Nevertheless, it remains one of the great* **mysteries** *of the* **human organism**.

There is no *UNIVERSAL AGREEMENT* about the exact **composition** of the aura. **Scientific devices** are not yet sufficiently sensitive to determine precisely how many different layers the aura consists of, *while subjective and traditional accounts differ.* There might be as few as SEVEN and as many as TWELVE separate layers. The FUNCTIONS of the **subfields**, or "*bodies*," described on the following pages, however, are the subject of general agreement.

The Etheric Body

This field is the **electromagnetic** energy matrix of the **physical body** and consists of an energetic REPLICA of the body and its functions. Also known as the "*vital body*" or, more poetically, as the "*body electric*," it contains the *SUBTLE ANATOMY* that has long been recognized by EASTERN traditions.

- **Chakras**: Seven major energy centers that FILTER, TRANSFORM, and CONDUCT specific energetic qualities *corresponding to the planetary energies.*

- **Nadis**: Subtle energy channels that CONNECT the chakras and TRANSMIT their energies.

- **Meridians**: A network of channels that CIRCULATE energy all over the body. (*See pages 138–139 for more detail.*)

AWARENESS of the etheric body and the etheric universe can be awakened by *MEDITATION, YOGA, and certain SHAMANISTIC practices.* **The etheric body consists of two auric layers**. The FIRST extends about 1 foot (30 centimeters) from the physical body and is exactly the SAME SHAPE. The SECOND extends about 3 feet (1 meter) or more and is less clearly defined. *The inner level is the easiest of the auric fields to see.* It has a LUMINOUS, SPARKLING quality; its colors vary from **blue** and **silver** to **violet**.

The Emotional Body

The etheric body derives its **consciousness** from the more refined emotional body, to which it provides ENERGY. *The emotional body corresponds to the* "heart"*—the seat of the* EMOTIONS, LIKES, DISLIKES, TASTES, *and* ESTHETIC APPRECIATIONS. Your emotions color your responses and drive your desire for **dominance** and **power**, as well as your **yearning** for *LOVE, PEACE*, and *SECURITY*. The emotional body is **easily damaged** by negative experiences and indulging in negative emotional states, such as ENVY, HATE, and SELF-PITY. **Diseases** will often become manifest in the emotional body, *and LEAKS from the emotional body can attract PREDATORS from the astral plane.* The emotional body is balanced by **unconditional love**.

The colors of the emotional body are CHANGEABLE and tend to reflect someone's dominant emotional characteristics: *dull RED for an* **angry** *type, GREENISH for a* **jealous** *type, BLUE for a* **soulful** *type, and YELLOW for a* **thinker**. Humans are far more sensitive to changes in the emotional body than they think. When you say someone is "*incandescent with rage*" or "*green with envy*," you are giving an ACCURATE DESCRIPTION of the emotional body.

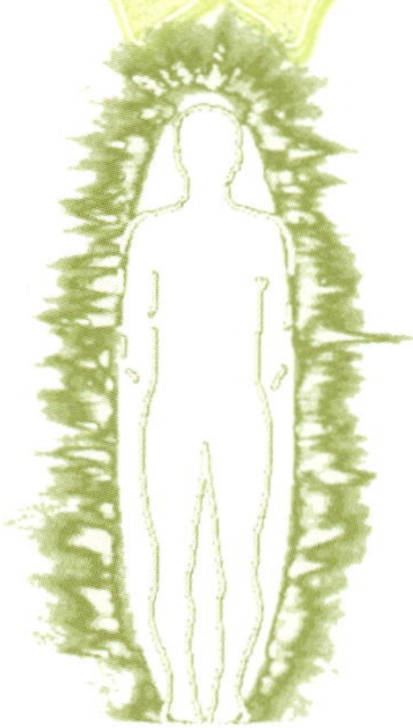

The Astral Body

The astral body is often confused with the emotional body. Although they shade into one another, they are in fact quite *DISTINCT*. The linking factor is **desire**. The astral body is occasionally called the "*desire body*" because it connects you with the **astral plane**—*a REAL, yet IMAGINED, world that you experience subjectively, as if in a DREAM*, where you are driven by your desires and needs. OUT-OF-BODY and NEAR-DEATH experiences occur on the astral level, as do VISIONS, HALLUCINATIONS, and VISIONARY DREAMS. This is the psychic level accessible to the following **extrasensory** abilities.

- **Clairvoyance**: The ability to see things beyond the range of normal human vision.

- **Clairaudience**: The ability to hear things outside the normal human range of hearing.

- **Psychometry** (*remote viewing*): The ability to discern events connected with things and places.

Meditation, out-of-body experiences, shamanic practices, lucid dreaming, entheogenic drugs, and certain types of psychological experiences will AWAKEN your awareness of the astral universe. When you **visit** the astral realm, you may **meet** all manner of **other beings** operating, such as GHOSTS and other SPIRITS, *as well as the astral bodies of other living people.* Your inner astral body is the same shape and size as your physical body. It has an **almond-shaped aura** extending 4–10 feet (1–3 meters) from your body. Its colors CHANGE with your MOODS.

The Mental Body

The mental or INTELLECTUAL body is the vehicle of the mind principle within the physical universe. *It governs* **cognition***—the FACULTY of KNOWING.* It allows you to think and discern, to **formulate** CONCEPTS and BELIEFS. All knowledge is accessed through this realm. *Mental consciousness enables you to TRANSLATE the information provided by your senses into* **concrete ideas of reality**. It allows you to *DISCERN DETAIL* and **analyze** things both in isolation and in context. *It covers the full range of thinking, from the PRECISE, SPECIFIC, and CONCRETE to the* **general**, **abstract**, *and* **intuitive**. The mental plane governs REASON, LOGIC, INTUITION, MEMORY, and the faculty of SPEECH. Awareness of the mental plane is stimulated by **academic study** and intellectual pursuits. It is often described as YELLOW in color, less structured than the etheric body, *and OVOID in shape like the aura of the astral body.*

The Soul Body

This is also known as the "*causal body,*" because the soul, as your *INCARNATE IDENTITY*, brings with it **karmic patterns** carried over from previous lifetimes, *which have an immediate effect on the CAUSE-AND-EFFECT DYNAMIC of your life*. That is to say, **your soul reflects all your predispositions**. It is the source of both CHARACTER and PERSONALITY by which and through which you relate to life and life relates to you. *It is what causes you to be here at all and represents your ESSENTIAL IDENTITY.* When you die, the immortal part of you is **reabsorbed** into the soul body. The soul body surrounds you like a GOLDEN SUN, *whose brightness depends on your level of MATURITY*. The aura of a **highly evolved soul** can RADIATE up to 30 feet (10 meters) from the body.

The Auric Envelope

The auric envelope surrounds and contains the auric bodies. It shields you from negative energies and prevents energy leakages. Ill-health and damaging environmental factors, such as radiation, can weaken or even fracture your auric envelope, allowing unhealthy influences to enter and causing imbalances in your auric fields. Fractures will also allow energy to leak out of your aura, causing tiredness, depression, and a weakened immune system. Such leakages may also attract energy parasites.

Strengthening Your Aura

Your **auric shield** *protects and sustains you in the same way as the* ATMOSPHERE *sustains the planet* EARTH. If your aura becomes *WEAK*, you will be more *SUSCEPTIBLE* to *OCCULT ATTACK*. By strengthening your aura, you can PROTECT yourself from MALICIOUS MAGIC and improve your sense of general well-being. Methods of doing this include **exercise**, **meditation**, and **yoga**, *which are discussed in the following chapters.*

Chapter 3

Building Your Magic Shield

Whether or not you SUSPECT that you or someone you know may be in DANGER of **occult attack**, it is wise to take **basic precautions** against psychic interference. *In addition to protecting the* FRIENDS *or* FAMILY *members with whom you live*, the measures given here will **improve** your QUALITY of LIFE.

Sacred Space

If you are to develop your own *POWERFUL MAGICAL SHIELD, you have to be convinced that it is your* **inviolable right** *to be protected from any kind of OCCULT INTERFERENCE.* All humans have a right to their own sacred space, **safe from intrusion**. This includes your physical and energy bodies, as well as your IMMEDIATE ENVIRONMENT—your home. *Although this is a UNIVERSAL LAW*, it is also a FACT of NATURE that all living beings above the order of plants FEED off others. This even applies to HERBIVORES and VEGETARIANS because plants, too, are living beings. **Plants** *have highly developed individual RESPONSE SYSTEMS that show that they have a degree of awareness.* They, too, have defense systems, *ensuring that PREDATORS attack the WEAKER members of their species,* **allowing the strongest to thrive**.

You, too, owe it to yourself to become as strong as possible in order to **resist** SPIRITUAL ATTACK. *The name of the game is* **survival**. Setting aside all considerations of good and evil for a moment, *the spirits and negative entities that operate on the astral plane need* **sustenance**. Their BEHAVIOR is governed by their need to survive. They must take energy wherever they can find it, *but YOU SHOULD NOT ALLOW them to take it from you.*

The Outer Magic Shield

THE FIRST THING YOU HAVE TO DO IS TO SHORE UP YOUR IMMEDIATE DEFENSES IN ORDER TO GIVE YOURSELF THE SPACE TO GROW STRONGER. YOUR HOME SHOULD BE CLEARED OF NEGATIVE ENERGY, PROVIDING YOU WITH A SAFE ENVIRONMENT CONDUCIVE TO POSITIVE CHANGE.

Spring Cleaning

The first thing to do in order to PROTECT your HOME from unwelcome intrusion is to **clear it of any stagnant energy**. *This involves a THOROUGH RITUAL CLEANING of your home from top to bottom. Choose a bright, airy day.* **Put on old clothes**, roll up your sleeves, and *ARM YOURSELF* with the **weaponry** of cleanliness: MOP, BROOM, DUSTER, CLOTH, SCRUBBING BRUSH, BUCKET, and VACUUM CLEANER.

SWEEP OUT every dark corner, **chase out every cobweb**, SCRUB the floors, CLEAN the windows, and WASH the carpets, the curtains, and the upholstery. *Dust every surface and polish everything in sight.* Do it *JOYFULLY* and *PURPOSEFULLY*. **Play music**, clash cymbals, laugh, and sing. *Throw your WINDOWS open wide and let in as much LIGHT as possible.* Let the fresh air circulate freely and blow away everything fusty and musty. **Follow your exertions with a ritual bath**. Light some candles, add your favorite essential oils, and wash away all impurities from MIND, BODY, and SPIRIT. *Afterward, rub your aching muscles with soothing* **St. John's wort oil**.

FUMIGATION

Once you have cleaned your physical space thoroughly, you should **purify** its energy with **smoke**. Shut all the windows and sprinkle a mixture of raw FRANKINCENSE (*olibanum*) and MYRRH onto burning coals in a CENSER (*available from church supply stores*). These **sacred resins** are used throughout the world for purification rituals. *Swing the censer to make sure the smoke gets into every NOOK and CRANNY of every room.* Air the room afterward.

Another fumigation method is **smudging**. This is a traditional NATIVE AMERICAN form of incense purification using a **tightly tied bundle of herbs** (*usually white sage*), known as a smudge stick. *LIGHT* the end and let it *CATCH* well before *BLOWING* it out and *WAFTING* and *BLOWING* the **purifying smoke** everywhere within reach.

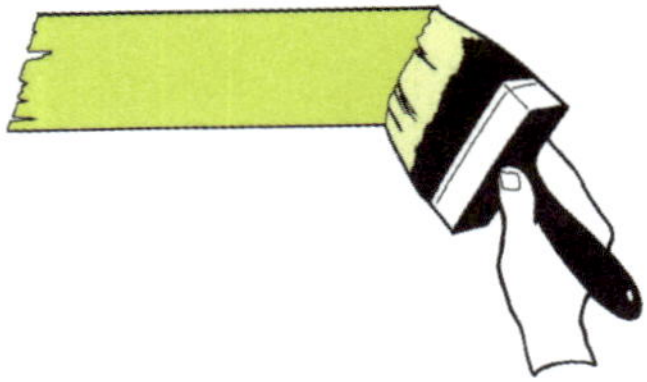

Salt

When your home is completely clean and cleared, **sprinkle some salt**, ideally CONSECRATED salt (*see pages 186–187*), around the rooms, especially in the corners. SALT, being crystalline, **absorbs negative energies**. *Some magicians scrub the walls and floors with salt water.* A fresh coat of **paint** on the walls does wonders for a room and is worth the *TROUBLE* and *EXPENSE*. Choose light, cheerful colors. *Negative energies accumulate in places that are DARK and MOODY.*

Water

Like salt, **water absorbs negative energy**. *Left out in bowls, it can clear the atmosphere in a room.* This is greatly enhanced if the water is consecrated (*see pages 186–187*) and mixed with ROSEWATER or a few drops of an essential oil like **rosemary** or **lavender**. Placed under the **bed** at night, water can help prevent **night terrors**. An ingenious way of protecting your home would be to run a narrow plastic tube (*like one used in fish tanks*) around the entire house to form a complete circle at ground level. *By attaching the tube to a small AQUARIUM WATER PUMP*, you can have a continuous **protective circle** of RUNNING WATER around your home. *Tubes and pumps can be bought from pet stores.*

Protective Objects

You can decorate your home with objects that are both PROTECTIVE and ATTRACTIVE. **Religious icons**, statuary, and charged amulets are particularly effective (*see pages 144–155*). *Religious objects are connected to the divine forces they symbolize.* They can RADIATE divine energy, particularly if you revere them and keep them clean. *CROSSES, CRUCIFIXES, ICONS, BUDDHAS, and other DEITIES can all work their magic.*

CRYSTALS, gems, and favorite objects are also protective. *Crystals and stones should be washed every so often in RUNNING WATER to clear them.* Freshwater streams are ideal. Traditionally, spirits do not like iron. An **iron horseshoe** set onto or over a door (*pointing upward*) is a well-known AMULET for **good luck** and **protection**.

A NOTE ABOUT SECOND-HAND ITEMS: ALL POSSESSIONS BEAR THE TRACE OF THEIR OWNERS, PARTICULARLY CLOTHING AND JEWELRY. THEY SHOULD BE CAREFULLY CLEANED TO CLEAR THEM OF UNWELCOME ENERGIES. THIS GOES FOR FAMILY HEIRLOOMS AS WELL. IMMERSE THEM IN CONSECRATED WATER OVERNIGHT.

Negative entities do not like music, particularly CLASSICAL MUSIC, INDIAN RAGAS, RELIGIOUS MUSIC, HYMNS, and CAROLS. *Playing such music, even quietly in the background, will help keep spirits at bay.* Tuning a RADIO into a classical music station and letting it PLAY CONSTANTLY in the background can be of great help.

The Inner Magic Shield

ONCE YOU HAVE TURNED YOUR HOME INTO A PROTECTED SACRED SPACE, YOU HAVE THE IDEAL ENVIRONMENT FOR WORKING ON YOURSELF AND CONSTRUCTING A POWERFUL MAGIC SHIELD. REVEL IN YOUR NEW SAFETY ZONE. FEEL GOOD, WARM, AND COMFORTABLE. YOU ARE NOW READY FOR A BETTER LIFE.

Making Changes

Make the changes to your lifestyle that you need to make. *Stop doing anything that may be making you VULNERABLE to attack.* If you have addictions, **address** them immediately. **Seek** professional help if necessary. It may be a LONG and DIFFICULT ROAD, but the sooner you get started, *the sooner you will be free.*

When trying to change your inner self, *it is a good idea to WITHDRAW from the outer world a little.* The more QUIETLY you can do this, the better. After all, you are trying to draw less attention to yourself, not more. You should **avoid** putting extra PRESSURE on yourself by trying to JUSTIFY or EXPLAIN your actions. Have the **courage** to say no to doing things you do not really want to do, *but make your excuses with a JOKE or a SMILE.*

Things to Avoid

Avoid bad company. People who have the same HABITS that you are trying to break are bound to be a **bad influence** if they are not ready to change. INSENSITIVE, SELFISH, EGOTISTICAL *people are not conducive to positive change.* **Avoid dangerous contacts**. People who are dabbling in the *OCCULT* can be carriers of negative energy, as can many people who purport to be *NEW AGE GURUS* and *SPIRITUAL GUIDES*. This is not a time to be exposing yourself to new outside influences. *A* **snake** *is most vulnerable when it is shedding its skin*; it needs to be SAFE in its DEN.

Be Moderate

Don't feel that you have to act too drastically. You don't have to *ABANDON* all your friends, *quit your job*, and *WITHDRAW* from the world *COMPLETELY*. Value the friends who really care about you, *and as for your job*, even if you do not find it especially **rewarding**, *if it pays the rent and keeps you fed*, you may as well stick with it rather than RISK the extra **stress** of **unemployment** or a change of career.

Fasting

Periods of fasting, ABSTINENCE *from stimulants and intoxicants,* and CHASTITY are all methods employed by the world's great religions to purify the inner self. MYSTICS, SAINTS, and DEVOUT FOLLOWERS of most religious traditions value periods of fasting as an opportunity for **purification** and **spiritual enlightenment**. CHRISTIANS observe *LENT*; MUSLIMS, *RAMADAN*; and JEWS, *YOM KIPPUR*. HINDUS *and* BUDDHISTS *also observe regular periods of ritual fasting.*

Observing any form of **abstinence** will help you **exorcise** your demons. *Fasting also helps* **detoxify** *your body,* while the discipline required to ignore HUNGER PANGS and CRAVINGS builds character and willpower. *However, you should be CAREFUL not to overdo abstinence,* and check with a QUALIFIED DOCTOR if you have any medical concerns or conditions. *If you weaken yourself with excessive bouts of* **self-denial**, you will only make yourself more vulnerable. You should start these things SLOWLY, *allowing your body to get used to the change.*

Detoxification

When starting to fast, *avoid food for one day and night once a week.* **Drink** plenty of *FLUIDS* throughout the day. **Herbal teas** are allowed, but natural **spring water** is ideal. You can also have a glass or two of **fruit juice**, but do not cheat by drinking rich drinks—*a BANANA MILKSHAKE is just eating without the chewing.* The point is to switch off the body's main engine and give your DIGESTIVE SYSTEM a chance to rest. *Allow your body the opportunity to DETOXIFY while you exercise your WILLPOWER.*

Self-discipline

Most humans are used to SATISFYING their hunger immediately. *You will find it interesting to observe how you react to SELF-DENIAL.* It takes a lot of **self-discipline** to say **no** to your most basic INSTINCTS and to your EGO. The ego is the part of you that is used to running the show on its own, *UNOBSERVED. It is likely to offer resistance and undermine your resolve.* For this reason, it is best to **pray** before starting a fast or at least STATE CLEARLY to yourself what you plan to do and why it is a good idea. This will help *DENY* the *TEMPTER* when it tries to PERSUADE you that the whole exercise is pointless and counterproductive. *WINNING these initial battles is CRUCIAL to developing your magic shield.*

Recapitulation

Unless you are good at SITTING QUIETLY, CONTEMPLATING, or MEDITATING, *it helps to keep your mind occupied while in retreat from the world*, particularly when fasting. An excellent exercise is to **write a confessional recapitulation of your life**. This should be done as HONESTLY and THOROUGHLY as possible.

Try to feel COMPASSION for the people who have wronged you, *as well as recognize when you have wronged others*. You cannot build a strong shield without **knowing yourself**. Anything you cannot admit to yourself remains unconscious. *Where you are* UNCONSCIOUS, *you are vulnerable*; where you are DEFENSIVE, you are closed. *The great thing about a magic shield is that it allows you to be completely open*; **completely yourself**, without FEAR. So spit it all out, **confess everything**, deal with everything, and let it go. *It's the only way to move on.*

Cause and Effect

Don't be too hard on yourself, though. We all make mistakes; we all let ourselves down from time to time. It is only by RECOGNIZING your WEAKNESSES that you can grow stronger. **It is better to be ashamed than to feel guilty**. GUILT is a fearful emotion that tries to hide itself. By admitting your guilt, you **transform** it into shame, which is honest and humble. *Humility is a state of grace that can afford you WONDERFUL REVELATIONS*. A good way to confront yourself and see where you have CONTRIBUTED to your own problems is to take the time every night, before you fall asleep, *to recapitulate the events of the day in reverse*. This **frees** you from OVERIDENTIFYING with your own BEHAVIOR and allows you to see the **patterns** of cause and effect in your life.

Self-Acceptance and Self-Reliance

Recapitulation isn't simply confessional. *It helps you understand how your actions and choices have led you to where you are now.* Try not to **blame** your situation on anything outside yourself. By blaming life or others for your misfortunes, *you ABROGATE responsibility and see yourself as a victim.* Remember that **the point of all this is not to be a victim**. In the end, you are nobody's problem but your own. The **magic shield** is wrought through UNDERSTANDING, ACCEPTANCE, and SELF-RELIANCE.

Getting Rid of Parasites

All things that MANIFEST on the material plane have their CORRELATING spirits. **Diseases** have their spirits and can **infest** you under the right conditions. *They can also be PROJECTED onto people through powerful* **black magic**. Other minor parasitic spirits can **invade** you if they have the chance. Their presence in your energy field can manifest itself physically in the form of INTERNAL PARASITES like **flukes** and **nematodes**.

In building a strong inner shield, *you must clear out your BODY just as you cleared out your HOME.* There are many **pharmaceutical purgatives** against parasites. Most of them have negative SIDE EFFECTS and none of them can get rid of all parasites. Fortunately, **Mother Nature** is there, as always, to help. *Certain natural plant remedies taken together can RID the body of PARASITES.* The **plant remedies** listed in the following regime are relatively easy to obtain, *but you should always consult a* QUALIFIED HERBALIST *before embarking on any regime.*

Wormwood

This BITTER HERB has been used to expel parasites for thousands of years. Its GERMAN name is **wermut**, which literally means "*fortitude.*" *The powdered herb can be taken in capsules.* **Dosage**: two "*00*" capsules THREE TIMES A DAY before meals for a period of NINE DAYS; *then six capsules once per week for three weeks.*

Cloves

This well-known AROMATIC SPICE takes its name from the LATIN for "*nail,*" due to its shape. It can "*nail*" almost any parasite. **Dosage**: one "*00*" capsule THREE TIMES A DAY before meals for the FIRST WEEK; *two capsules three times daily for the second week*; then five capsules *ONCE PER WEEK* for the *THIRD* and *FOURTH WEEKS.*

Green Walnut Hulls

This well-known **folk medicine** should be taken as an ALCOHOLIC TINCTURE of the FRESH GREEN HULLS for maximum effect. **Dosage**: *one teaspoon* (5 ml) *in half a glass of water once a day before meals for six days*; then two teaspoons (10 ml) for one day, *followed by two teaspoons* (10 ml) *once a week for three weeks.*

It would be best not to fast for the first week of this regime. *The weekly doses should then be taken on a* **nonfasting day**. The regime can be repeated once every six months to keep you **parasite-free**. The WALNUT TINCTURE is not so easy to obtain; *try an Internet search or consult your local herbalist.*

Physical Exercise

KUM NYE *are simple but little-known physical exercises that are part of the Tibetan healing tradition.* They are traditionally practiced for **rejuvenation** and **life extension**. They INCREASE the VITALITY of the organism on all levels, *reducing its vulnerability to psychic attack.* When practiced on a daily basis, they can help you develop a **core fitness** that restores and sustains the health of BODY, MIND, and SPIRIT. *They are BALANCING and HARMONIZING and generate a state of RELAXATION that is ideal for MEDITATION.*

KUM NYE *has much in common with yoga*, but **unlike yoga** it does not require a high degree of *FLEXIBILITY* and does not involve *UNFAMILIAR MUSCULAR STRETCHES.* There are many KUM NYE positions, but the following four are all you need to develop CORE FITNESS and BALANCE. *Begin each exercise by standing in a relaxed position for a few seconds, taking slow, deep breaths.* You should be **barefoot** and wear **loose-fitting clothing**.

Exercise One

1. Sit on the ground with your feet shoulder-width apart and flat on the floor. Look straight ahead.

2. Straighten you spine and raise your arms straight up to either side, level with your shoulders.

3. Bend your elbows to form an L shape, fingers pointing straight up and palms facing the sides of your head. Breathe slowly and deeply and hold the position for as long as you can.

4. Relax, lower your arms, and stand up.

Exercise Two

1. With your feet shoulder-width apart and your toes pointing forward, sink down onto your haunches.

2. Clasp your hands and place your elbows inside your knees. Push up onto your toes, hands pointing forward, and look straight ahead.

3. Breathe slowly and deeply and hold the position for as long as you can.

4. Relax and push back up into a standing position.

Exercise Three

1. Lie flat on your stomach. Bring your hands together under your solar plexus, palms flat on the ground, and your thumbs and index fingers touching each other to form a heart shape.

2. Push up with your hands until your arms are straight and your whole body is supported on your hands and toes. Your toes should be pointing straight back, so that you are resting on your toenails. Hold your body in a straight line from neck to heels.

3. Look straight ahead and try to keep your breathing slow and steady. Hold for as long as you can, then slowly lower your body to the floor.

Exercise Four

1. *Stand with your feet shoulder-width apart, toes pointing forward.*

2. *Raise your arms to your sides, level with your shoulders, palms facing down.*

3. *Look straight ahead and then roll your eyeballs upward to look at the ceiling without moving your head.*

4. *Push out from your fingertips. Breathe slowly and deeply and hold the position for as long as you can.*

5. *Relax and lower your arms. You may find that they are most comfortable palms joined over your heart in a prayer position. Let your eyes, head, and shoulders relax and let any tension and emotion flow away from you. These exercises can touch deep parts of your soul and release a great deal of pent-up emotion. This is a positive effect, and you should allow it to happen.*

Chapter 4
Mantras and Meditations

In the SEMITIC TRADITION, believers use **prayer** to commune with the *DIVINE WILL*. The followers of HINDUISM and BUDDHISM employ other techniques, *including yoga, meditation, and the repetition of holy sounds*—MANTRAS—as paths to **self-knowledge** and **inner harmony**. The daily practice of *MEDITATION* techniques and *MANTRAS* will help you develop one the most powerful forms of **psychic self-protection**.

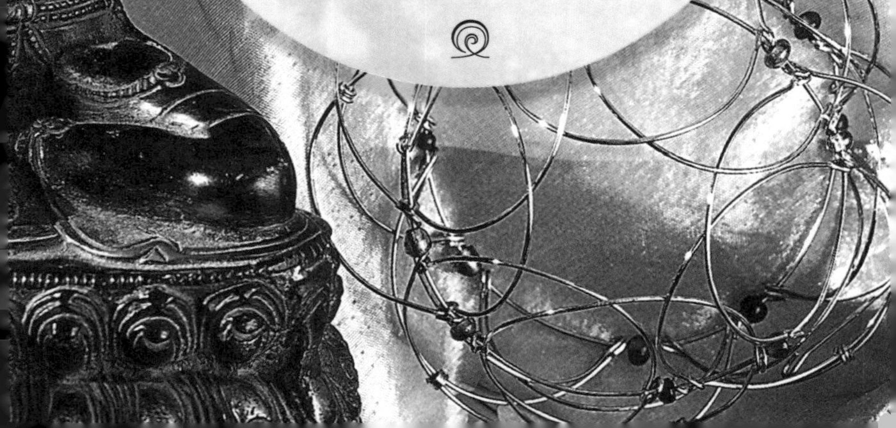

Prayer

PRAYER is the easiest way to establish contact with the DIVINE. Most people who pray regularly **believe** they are **communicating** directly with a PERSONAL DEITY. *This is the TRADITION of prayer that is found in the* SEMITIC *faiths.* The followers of other faiths believe that prayer will *ATTUNE* them to an immanent DIVINE PRINCIPLE. There are also those who believe that they are praying to their own *HIGHER SELF. The crucial shared element of all these beliefs is* **faith**. It is faith in the POWER of PRAYER that makes it so effective on both the INNER and OUTER PLANES.

Achieving Inner Calm

The elements of prayer include PRAISE, THANKSGIVING, CONFESSION *of* SIN, INTERCESSION *on behalf of others, and* SUPPLICATION. Acknowledging the existence of a HIGHER CONSCIOUSNESS helps to curb our self-importance; **confessing** *our wrongdoing and shortcomings helps us* **develop** *the SELF-KNOWLEDGE that we need to achieve a higher consciousness*; praying for others bestows on us the **special grace** engendered by **compassion**; *and SUPPLICATION helps us to express our highest desires.* Perhaps the most important element of prayer is the acceptance of the **divine will**. *This promotes a* **humility** *that can allow MIRACLES to occur.* The INNER CALM that regular prayer brings is an *IDEAL PRELUDE* to the practice of meditation, *through which you will achieve an even more PROFOUND STATE of* **equilibrium**.

Meditation

There are many forms of meditation, most of which are drawn from spiritual or religious traditions. The following technique is a good starting point, because it is a passive meditation that promotes well-being and inner equilibrium. The traditional position for meditating in Western magic is the "PHARAOH" *or* "EGYPTIAN GOD POSTURE."

1. On a STRAIGHT-BACKED CHAIR or STOOL, sit with your BACK straight, *your* FEET *flat on the floor,* and your PALMS on your thighs.

2. Close your eyes. Without forcing the **breath**, *INHALE slowly and smoothly for a count of four and HOLD your breath for a count of four.* Again without straining, *EXHALE for a count of four and HOLD the breath for a final count of four.* This constitutes **one breath cycle**.

3. Continue breathing in cycles as you **focus** your mind in the SOLAR PLEXUS, *a point in your body just below your breastbone.* This is the primary seat of consciousness that **connects** you to your EMOTIONAL STATES. *It is also the seat of your INNER LIGHT.* Feel the warmth of this light **spreading** out from your solar plexus and throughout your body.

At first you may find it difficult to **relax** enough to meditate but you should *PERSEVERE.* Your **ego** may feel uncomfortable as you begin to recognize *the unseen PUPPET STRINGS that control your behavior* and you begin to assert **self-control** for the first time. The greater your inner balance, *the more difficult it will be for external agencies to disturb you.* As a beginner, it can take up to SIX WEEKS of **daily practice** before you begin to experience a PROFOUND MEDITATIVE STATE.

The Caduceus

The technique described on the previous page is a **passive** MEDITATION. *However, to reach higher levels of consciousness,* it will be necessary to employ **active** MEDITATION techniques that consist of **creative** MENTAL EXERCISES. HERMES TRISMEGISTUS, *patron of all the magical arts,* offers us a key to achieving a magical inner balance known as **equipoise**.

Symbolism

This key is his **magic wand**, known as the CADUCEUS—*a central wand or pole around which two* **serpents** *are intertwined,* often surmounted by a pair of wings. The *INTERTWINED SNAKES* represent the **binary principles** at work in the manifest universe: MALE/FEMALE, LIGHT/DARK, GOOD/EVIL, or in Chinese philosophy, YIN/YANG. The central wand represents the **axis** between HEAVEN and EARTH—*the above and below.* It is also the symbol of the ONE as CREATOR and the balancing point between polarities; *the* **wings** *represent TRANSCENDENT consciousness.*

Origins

According to GREEK mythology, HERMES *came upon two snakes fighting.* He thrust his **staff** between them and they **coiled** around it. *The staff both DIVIDED and UNITED them,* preventing them from striking one other. Thus the CADUCEUS became the symbol of the *MESSENGER GOD, the divine herald who mediates between HEAVEN and EARTH and keeps them in* **balance**. A symbol of PEACE and PROTECTION, it is also used to represent the **medical arts**. *Above all, it represents the unity achieved through the reconciliation of opposites.* The Caduceus is an ancient symbol that probably first appeared in MESOPOTAMIA over 5,000 years ago. From there it found its way west to the Mediterranean world and east to INDIA. *It is in Indian yoga that the Caduceus is integrated as a* **living function** *within the human body.*

Yoga

Yoga refers to a wide range of SPIRITUAL DISCIPLINES in HINDUISM. *Their common aim is the* **mystical union** *of the self with the divine.* The HERMETIC ARTS are often described as WESTERN YOGA, since their aims are the same as those of INDIAN YOGA. *There are many different forms of yoga* but the system most commonly practiced in the WEST is HATHA YOGA, *known as* **the path of inner power**. In HATHA YOGA, *the body is PURIFIED and TONED through the* **asanas**, *or physical postures,* so that the mind and spirit can attain *HARMONY* and *BALANCE.* In addition to the *ASANAS,* HATHA YOGA uses **pranayama** breathing exercises to rouse the *VITAL ENERGY* known as **kundalini**.

KUNDALINI

Kundalini means **serpent power**, *because it is represented as a SLEEPING SNAKE coiled around the base of the spine.* Using **pranayama** techniques, *KUNDALINI ENERGY* is awakened and starts to rise up the SPINE. As it rises, it confers **supernatural powers** and **increased consciousness**. *With sufficient application it can be RAISED to the top of the spine and into the* **brain**, leading to a state of SUPREME CONSCIOUSNESS equated with *DIVINE UNION.*

Nadis

The subtle energy, or *PRANA, travels within the body through channels known as the* **nadis**. These are similar, though not identical, to the **meridians** used in TRADITIONAL CHINESE ACUPUNCTURE. Three of the main *NADIS* work together in the manner of the Caduceus. *The nadis known as the* IDA *and* PINGALA *coil around the central nadi known as the* SUSHUMNA. The Pingala is called the **Sun** channel—*being masculine and solar*—while the Ida is the **Moon** channel—*being feminine and lunar.* The Pingala runs from the left TESTICLE in men or the left side of the VULVA in women to the right NOSTRIL, *while the Ida takes the PARALLEL COURSE.* The Sushumna is simultaneously a **solar** and **lunar** channel and contains an inner nadi called the *BRAHMA NADI, which is the CHANNEL for the kundalini serpent power.*

Chakras

The **seven points** along the SUSHUMNA where the IDA and the PINGALA intersect are known as the **chakras**. These are the body's energy centers, *which can be EQUATED to the PLANETARY CENTERS from the Western esoteric tradition.* Indeed, each chakra has energies comparable to those of the classical planets. This is an example of the DOCTRINE of the MICROCOSM, which states that *every individual contains the whole universe.* As the serpent power is raised, **it opens each chakra in turn**. This is similar to the KABBALISTIC concept of the SOUL *mastering the energies of each planetary sphere* on its return to the divine source.

Caduceus Meditation

The correlation between the **Caduceus** and the **nadis** is the basis of a very powerful ACTIVE MEDITATION technique. This exercise is unlikely to awaken **kundalini** on its own, *but it is nevertheless very effective in helping you achieve magical equipoise.* Sit as before in the EGYPTIAN GOD POSTURE described on page 136, or in the traditional **crossed-legged yoga pose** shown here.

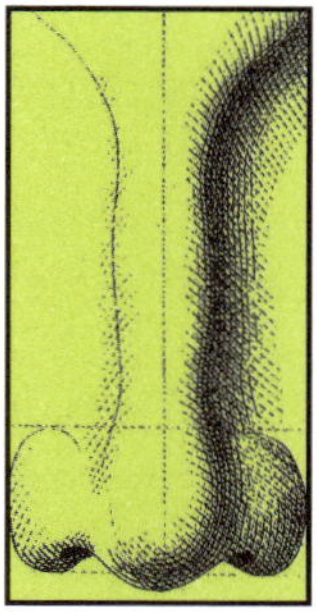

1. When you have CALMED your MIND and BREATHING, concentrate on the **root** chakra (*located at the base of the spine between the anus and the sexual organs*). Bring your attention up along the *SUSHUMNA*, *focusing on the remaining six chakras in turn*: PELVIC, SOLAR PLEXUS, HEART, THROAT, THIRD EYE (*middle of forehead*), and CROWN.

2. When you have reached the **crown** chakra, focus on the *PINGALA—the solar channel*—breathing through the **right nostril** (*block the left nostril*) and following its course from base to crown as you **inhale**. HOLD your BREATH at the crown for a *COUNT* of *FOUR*. Follow the *PINGALA* down as you **exhale**.

3. Follow the same instructions for the *IDA—the lunar channel—* but this time **block** you right nostril and **breathe** through the channel with your **left nostril**.

4. With **regular practice**, you will become aware of your chakras and you will feel the nadis RESONATING and CIRCULATING the **prana** within you. When you feel that their energies are in balance, *focus your attention on the* SUSHUMNA. Feel the power flowing up your **spine**, *giving you the poise and presence of a SAMURAI WARRIOR*. In this state you will be able to shield yourself from any INTERFERENCE; *you will have become your own* **magic shield**.

Mantras

*"IN THE BEGINNING WAS THE WORD,
AND THE WORD WAS GOD."*

This **tenet** of the JUDEO-CHRISTIAN faith is echoed in the HINDU tradition, which holds that the **material universe** (JAGAT) was created by divine vibration. JAGAT means "*that which moves,*" because everything at its most fundamental level is an AMALGAM of MOVING FORCES. The tiniest atom is **constantly vibrating**, *creating its own sound.* Thus everything has its own **sonic signature**, which is its true or "*natural*" name. *These subtle vibrations find corresponding ECHOES in SPEECH.* Everything is therefore CONNECTED through LANGUAGE.

Natural Names

This concept of natural names lies at the HEART of MAGIC. *To be able to* **utter** *the natural name of a thing is to be able to CONTROL it or even MANIFEST it.* When the LORD JEHOVAH gave MOSES the *TRUE* name of **water** in the **desert**, Moses uttered it and water *GUSHED* forth. ADAM was given the task of naming everything in CREATION. By uttering their true names, *he brought all things into being.* The ABORIGINALS of AUSTRALIA have a similar concept, as did the CELTIC DRUIDS. This explains why people were once so superstitious about letting a **fingernail** or even a single **hair** fall into the wrong hands, *because they FEARED that a powerful* **sorcerer** *could use these items to determine their individual VIBRATORY SIGNATURE and find a means of* CONTROLLING *them.*

A-U-M

All **spells** and **incantations** are based on the concept that certain words have INNATE POWER because of their close *CORRESPONDENCE* to specific forces. In HINDUISM and BUDDHISM, *sounds that have divine power are known as* **mantras**. The BEST-KNOWN mantra is the *TRI-SYLLABLE* "A-U-M," known to us as "OM." This is associated with the *PROCESSES* of *CREATION* and is the basis of the letters of the sacred language of HINDUISM, **Sanskrit**. The KABBALAH has a similar concept because HEBREW is also a **sacred language**.

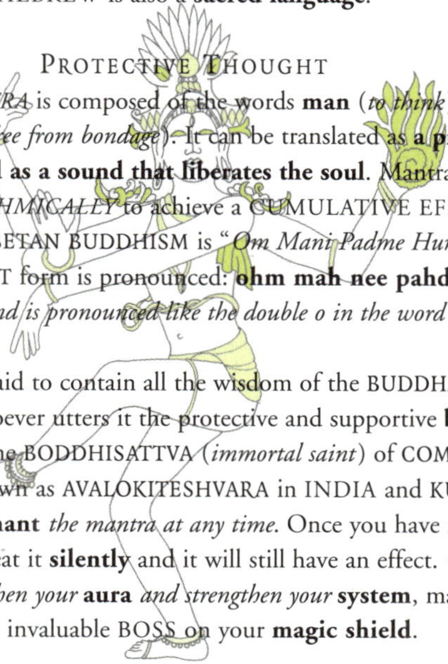

Protective Thought

The word *MANTRA* is composed of the words **man** (*to think*) and **trai** (*to protect or to free from bondage*). It can be translated as **a protective thought expressed as a sound that liberates the soul**. Mantras are often *REPEATED RHYTHMICALLY* to achieve a CUMULATIVE EFFECT. The classic mantra of TIBETAN BUDDHISM is "*Om Mani Padme Hum*," which in its original SANSKRIT form is pronounced: **ohm mah nee pahd may hoom** (*the last oo sound is pronounced like the double o in the word room*).

This mantra is said to contain all the wisdom of the BUDDHA and to bestow upon whoever utters it the protective and supportive **blessings** of CHENREZIG, the BODDHISATTVA (*immortal saint*) of COMPASSION. CHENREZIG is known as AVALOKITESHVARA in INDIA and KUAN-YIN in CHINA. *You can* **chant** *the mantra at any time.* Once you have mastered it, you can even repeat it **silently** and it will still have an effect. *Over time it will strengthen your* **aura** *and strengthen your* **system**, making it the invaluable BOSS on your **magic shield**.

Chapter 5

AMULETS

Down the ages people of all **cultures** have used similar techniques to **protect** themselves from SORCERERS and other NEGATIVE INFLUENCES. The most common technique is the use of **amulets**. *Even in Western societies it is still common to give people about to go on a journey a* ST. CHRISTOPHER *medallion to* **protect** *them.* ST. CHRISTOPHER was chosen to be the **patron saint of travelers** because he carried JESUS over the *FLOODWATERS*.

Sympathetic Magic

The **principle** upon which all magic is founded is "*like affects like.*" The RIGHT NOTE at the RIGHT PITCH will *SHATTER GLASS*. When magical practitioners want to affect someone or something in a certain way, they must **strike** the *RIGHT NOTE* by "*tuning into*" the object of their **intent**. *To help them do this*, they may use or create objects that connect them to the *INTENDED RECIPIENT*.

Vibrational Signature

If the practitioner has a **hair** or a **fingernail** from the person concerned, then he or she has a *DIRECT CONNECTION*, because the part and the whole share the same vibrational signature. *An article of* **clothing** *or a piece of* **jewelry** *can also establish a strong link*; a **photograph** is ideal. If the magical practitioner cannot get a personal item, *he or she can make an* **effigy** *of the person* and treat it in such a way that certain effects are **transmitted** onto it.

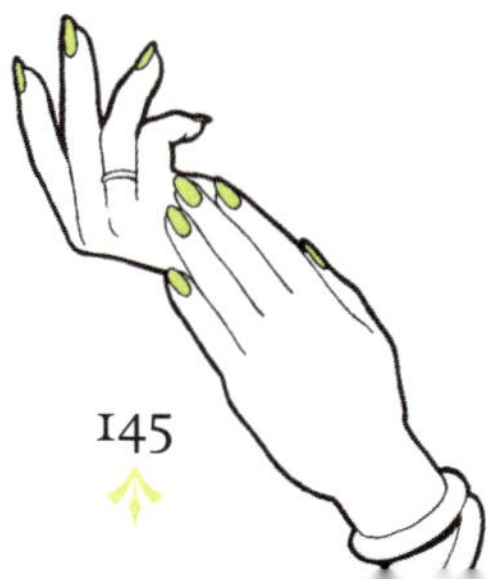

Planetary Archetypes

The LAW of CORRESPONDENCES exemplifies the great HERMETIC AXIOM: "*As above, so below.*" Everything in our solar system has the *SAME SOURCE—from the* **planets** *down to the smallest* **creatures** *and specks of* **dust**. As the PRINCIPAL BODIES of the system, **the planets represent the seven great archetypes of being**. *This is not mere convention.* It has been *SCIENTIFICALLY PROVEN* that the planets have a specific **affinity** with the METALS with which they are *CLASSICALLY CONNECTED*. So, too, all things in nature have special affinities with particular planets.

Ruling Planets

This **law** applies to HUMAN BEINGS as well—*each one of us is* **attuned** *to one particular planet.* Astrology **teaches** that we all have a *RULING PLANET. This is DETERMINED by the sign of the* **zodiac** *under which we were born.* In classical magic and astrology, SATURN, JUPITER, MARS, VENUS, and MERCURY *each rule two of the zodiac signs,* while the *SUN* and the *MOON* each rule one.

Aries	*Mars*
Taurus	*Venus*
Gemini	*Mercury*
Cancer	*Moon*
Leo	*Sun*
Virgo	*Mercury*
Libra	*Venus*
Scorpio	*Mars*
Sagittarius	*Jupiter*
Capricorn	*Saturn*
Aquarius	*Saturn*
Pisces	*Jupiter*

Correspondences

To help you SELECT the OBJECTS that you can use to make **amulets** or **charm pouches**, *use the correspondences of your ruling planet.* For example, if your ruling planet is JUPITER, you could make your charm pouch out of DEERSKIN, *dyed blue*, and fill it with the following objects: a whole *NUTMEG*, a piece of *LAPIS LAZULI*, a *HORSE CHESTNUT*, a piece of *GINSENG*, or a piece of *COMFREY ROOT*. All these things are **ruled** by the planet Jupiter and have a special AFFINITY *with those born under the* **two zodiac signs** *under its* RULERSHIP.

SATURN

SATURN *is the farthest of the classical planets.* **Identified** by the *ANCIENT GREEKS* as the god CHRONOS (from whom we derive the word "*chronology*"), Saturn **rules** the material realm of *TIME* and *SPACE*, which is why it is often **personified** as "*Old Father Time.*" Saturn's **virtues** are DISCIPLINE, PERSEVERANCE, SINCERITY, and WISDOM; its **vices** are *MELANCHOLY*, *CRANKINESS*, and *INFLEXIBILITY.*

Keyword: *Saturnine*
Colors: *Iridescent black, purple*
Day: *Saturday*
Zodiac signs: *Aquarius, Capricorn*
Number: *Three*
Shape: *Triangle*
Metal: *Lead*

Creatures: *Ant, beaver, mole, termite, tortoise, vole*
Stones: *Black coral, diamond, granite, jet, obsidian, onyx*
Incense: *Aloe, copal, harmal, myrrh, spikenard*
Trees: *Beech, holly, poplar, Scots pine, yew*
Healing plants: *Comfrey, equisetum, heartsease, red root, uva ursi*

JUPITER

Jupiter is the **largest** of the visible planets. In classical mythology, *it represented the king of the OLYMPIAN GODS*—the ZEUS of the *GREEKS* and JUPITER of the *ROMANS. Where SATURN is restrictive, JUPITER* is EXPANSIVE, WARM, and GENEROUS, which is why it is known as "*the harbinger of joy.*" Too great an **influence** from Jupiter, however, *can make one* **self-indulgent** *with a TENDENCY to EXCESS.*

Keyword: *Jovial*
Colors: *Blue, mauve, purple*
Day: *Thursday*
Zodiac signs: *Pisces, Sagittarius*
Number: *Four*
Shape: *Square*
Metals: *Tin, zinc*
Creatures: *Bee, deer, dolphin, eagle, elephant, fish, horse, water birds, whale*
Stones: *Amethyst, lapis lazuli, sapphire, tanzanite, topaz, turquoise*
Incense: *Benzoin, cedar, fennel, gum mastic, myrrh, nutmeg, sandalwood*
Trees: *Ash, cedar, horse chestnut, maple, oak*
Healing plants: *Arnica, borage, comfrey, echinacea, ginseng, lemon balm, sage*

MARS

The RED PLANET is the **warrior** of the solar system *and was the ancients' god of war.* It represents the MASCULINE, ACTIVE, and DYNAMIC principle of life. DETERMINATION, WILLPOWER, COURAGE, and PASSION are its chief **virtues**, while its **vices** include *DESTRUCTIVENESS, BRUTALITY,* and *RUTHLESSNESS.*

Keyword: *Martial*
Color: *Red*

Day: *Tuesday*
Zodiac signs: *Aries, Scorpio*
Number: *Five*
Shape: *Pentagon*
Metal: *Iron*
Creatures: *Pike, ram, scorpion, stinging insects (except bees), vulture, wolf*
Stones: *Bloodstone, carnelian, garnet, ruby*
Incense: *Aloe, cypress, pine, red cedar, tobacco*
Trees: *Cypress, pine, rhododendron, savin, thorn trees*
Healing plants: *Basil, hawthorn, monkshood, nettle, onion, sarsaparilla, vomic nut*

THE SUN

The Sun—*the god* APOLLO—is the **radiant heart** of the solar system, *whose* LIGHT *and* WARMTH *sustains all life*. The Sun rules INDIVIDUALITY, CONSCIOUSNESS, and VITALITY. *Without the COOLING, MOISTENING influence of the Moon*, however, the Sun can be **arid** and **burning**. Excessive solar influence can lead to VANITY and EGOTISM.

Keyword: *Solar*
Colors: *Gold, yellow*
Day: *Sunday*
Zodiac sign: *Leo*
Number: *Six*
Shape: *Hexagon*
Metal: *Gold*
Creatures: *Blackbird, butterflies (yellow and orange), cat, lion, swan*
Stones: *Amber, carbuncle, chrysolite ruby, tiger's eye*
Incense: *Bergamot, cinnamon, clove, frankincense (olibanum), myrrh*
Trees: *Ash, citrus, juniper, laurel, walnut*
Healing plants: *Chamomile, eyebright, rosemary, St. John's wort*

Venus

Venus is the GODDESS of LOVE. *She is the muse of ART, FRIENDSHIP, and MUSIC*, and **inspires** AFFECTION and INTIMACY. An exaggeration of the Venusian principle leads to an **excess** of WANTONNESS and LUST.

Keyword: *Relating*
Colors: *Emerald, rose*
Day: *Friday*
Zodiac signs: *Libra, Taurus*
Number: *Seven*
Shape: *Heptagon*
Metal: *Copper*
Creatures: *Butterfly, deer, dove, rabbit, swallow*
Stones: *Emerald, jade, malachite, opal, pink coral, rose quartz*
Incense: *Galbanum, rose, sandalwood, storax, valerian, violet*
Trees: *Apple, cherry, chestnut, elder, linden, pear*
Healing plants: *Lady's mantle, motherwort, vervain, yarrow*

Mercury

Mercury is the *FASTEST MOVING* of the planets. As the **herald** of the gods, MERCURY/HERMES *mediates between HEAVEN and EARTH.* Mercury **rules** TRAVEL, COMMUNICATIONS, LANGUAGE, WRITING, ADAPTABILITY, and the INTELLECT. There is an **ambivalent quality** to Mercury that can make it *TRICKY* and *UNRELIABLE.*

Keyword: *Mercurial*
Color: *Orange*
Day: *Wednesday*
Zodiac signs: *Gemini, Virgo*
Number: *Eight*

Shape: *Octagon*
Metal: *Quicksilver (mercury)*
Creatures: *Coyote, flies, ibis, monkey, raven, stork, trout*
Stones: *Carnelian, chalcedony, opal, peridot, smokey quartz, tourmaline*
Incense: *Anise, gum arabic, lavender, storax*
Trees: *Acacia, hazel, mulberry, myrtle*
Healing plants: *Caraway, digitalis, mandrake, parsley, skullcap, valerian, wormwood*

The Moon

The Moon is known as "*the Queen of the Deep.*" She represents the *FEMININE* principle and **rules** the EMOTIONS, INSTINCTS, and SUBCONSCIOUS. The Moon has the **governance of the fluids**, including the *OCEAN TIDES* and the *MENSTRUAL CYCLE*

Keyword: *Lunar*
Colors: *Royal purple, silver, violet*
Day: *Monday*
Zodiac sign: *Cancer*
Number: *Nine*
Shape: *Nonagon*
Metal: *Silver*
Creatures: *Moths, nightingale, nightjar, owl, seal, shellfish, spiders*
Stones: *Aquamarine, fluorite, moonstone, pearl*
Incense: *Camphor, jasmine, ylang-ylang*
Trees: *Magnolia, willow*
Healing plants: *Chaste tree, cleavers, opium poppy, periwinkle, watercress*

Making and Using Amulets

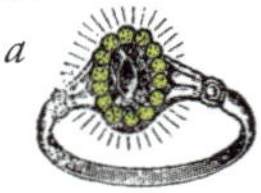

Amulets are very EASY to make. *The simplest do not even have to be made*; they just need to be "*energized*" or "*charged*." The **simplest** form of amulet is a CRYSTAL or STONE *carried in your pocket or* **worn** *as a PENDANT*. For a more specific or personal focus, *you can use one of the objects associated with your ruling planet that are listed in the* CORRESPONDENCES *on pages 147–151. PERSONAL ITEMS*, such as **jewelry**, make ideal amulets. ARTIFICIAL SUBSTANCES, *such as* **plastic**, *however, are very hard to CHARGE.*

Protective Stones

There are many stones **valued** for their protective qualities. One of the most traditional is SMOKY QUARTZ, while CLEAR QUARTZ is so **receptive** that it *READILY LENDS ITSELF* to any kind of **intent** when charged. Stones with **holes**, *particularly natural holes*, are considered *ESPECIALLY PROTECTIVE. They are also easy to hang from your* **neck**. Here is a list of some of the most widely used.

General protection: *Agate, clear quartz, fluorite, garnet, jade, malachite, onyx, sard, smoky quartz, turquoise*

Physical protection: *Coral, jet*

Psychic/spiritual protection: *Black tourmaline, labradorite, lapis lazuli*

Clearing the Stones

Stones should be **washed** and "*cleared*," as should all WATERPROOF ITEMS before being **charged** as amulets. *The best way to* **clear** *a stone is to place it in RUNNING WATER for a few moments.* A **freshwater stream** is best, or you could wash it in the **sea**, or even under a **faucet** if necessary. *The stone can then be placed in a glass of pure spring water* and placed in the SUN for a few moments to **imbue** it with SOLAR ENERGY, which is very **protective**.

Charging an Amulet

It is important to "*charge*," or "*energize*," your amulet to **activate** its PROTECTIVE POWERS. Once charged, *use your amulet* **immediately** *in the manner you have chosen.* You can **recharge** your *AMULET* in the same way any time you feel it is necessary. *A well-charged AMULET need only be recharged ONCE or TWICE a year at most.*

1. Hold your AMULET in your **receptive** hand (*left, if you are right-handed; or right, if you are left-handed*).

2. ENCLOSE the amulet *COMPLETELY* in your **hand** and *shut your eyes. Take a few deep* **breaths**, *then steady your breathing.*

3. As you breathe in, *imagine that you are summoning up your* **inner light** *and* **power**. As you BREATHE OUT, *sense your ENERGY flowing* CALMLY *but* POWERFULLY *from your* **solar plexus**, down your **arm**, into your **hand**, *and CHARGING the amulet.*

4. SENSE the amulet starting to PULSE with your *PERSONAL ENERGY, in time with your own* **heartbeat**, so that it becomes an *EXTENSION* of yourself.

5. IMAGINE the amulet as you would **wear** it, *quietly but powerfully pulsing with your energy and light, ACTING* as a **force field** to keep you aligned with your own power and free from outside disturbance. You can imagine any spiritual GUIDES, ALLIES, or DEITIES whom you **honor** *adding their light and energy to your amulet.*

6. When you **sense** that the amulet is *WELL CHARGED, take a* DEEP BREATH *and open your* **hand** *as you* **breathe out**.

Charm Pouches

Amulets *WORK BEST* if you **wear** them all the time. *You can wear them around your* NECK, WRIST, *or* ANKLE. Charm pouches, known as "*medicine bags*" among NATIVE AMERICANS, are perfect for **carrying** amulets. *If they are made carefully*, they can act as amulets themselves. They can be made out of any **pliant material**, *including* SILK *and* LEATHER.

1. TAKE a piece of your *CHOSEN MATERIAL and place your amulet in the* **center**.

2. DRAW the material up around the amulet and TIE a piece of STRING around the **neck** to *CREATE* a small POUCH or BAG.

3. MARK *a few points about* 1 inch (2.5 cm) *above the neck*, to show you how much **material** you will need to **cut off**. OPEN *the material and* CUT OUT *a* **circle** *defined by the points you have* **marked**.

4. MAKE *a few* **holes** *in the material about* ½ inch (1 cm) *from the* **edge**. *LOOP* a piece of RIBBON, CORD, or THONG through the holes.

5. PLACE the amulet in the *MIDDLE* of the *CLOTH* and DRAW the **string** tight enough to CLOSE the **pouch**.

6. TIE a **knot** to keep the **bag** *CLOSED* and *HANG* it from your **neck**.

Protective Plants

Many *PLANT VARIETIES* have been used since ANCIENT TIMES as **protective** amulets. *The* **dried leaves** *and* **roots** *are placed in a charm pouch that is WORN around the* **neck**. Here is a short list of the *BEST-KNOWN* plants with SOME of their **traditional uses**.

Angelica: *Used as incense or added to bath water to neutralize hexes.*

Ash: An ash staff placed over the doorway will protect a house.

Bay: *Burned as incense in exorcisms.*

Beans: These are used in rattles to rid people of minor spirits.

Comfrey: *The root protects travelers on the road.*

Ebony: One of the best woods for making wands.

Ferns: *Dried fern can be burned on hot coals to drive away evil spirits.*

Garlic: Eaten fresh to prevent evil spirits from entering. Whole bulbs hung in windows protect a dwelling.

Ginseng: *The root is burned in China as a hex-breaker.*

Heather: A sprig of heather is worn as an amulet against physical assault.

Holly: *A sprig of holly provides all-round protection.*

Lily: The flower gives protection when planted in the garden.

Lotus: *Inhaling the scent of the lotus protects against evil spirits.*

Mugwort: All parasitic entities hate the smell of this plant.

Oak: *Oak twigs bound with red thread to form an equal-armed cross are hung in a house for protection.*

Onion: A bulb stuck with pins and placed in a window prevents all evil from entering.

Orris: *This is added to bath water for all-round protection.*

Rose: The flower is worn for personal protection.

St. John's wort: *Use it during meditation to identify persecutors.*

Valerian: When this is drunk as a tea, it protects against night terrors.

Wormwood: *This protects vehicles from accidents when hung inside.*

Chapter 6

Talismans

The talisman is one of the most powerful **tools** for magical SELF-DEFENSE. The word TALISMAN is derived from the GREEK word *TELESMA*, meaning **ritual**, which is itself derived from the word *TELOS, meaning result or end. A talisman, therefore, is an object ritually prepared to achieve a specific result.* The ritual is designed to CHARGE the talisman with the **forces** and **qualities** that correspond to the MAGE'S AIMS.

Uses of Talismans

The difference between TALISMANS and AMULETS is that the latter are objects worn for **protection**, while the former can be MAGICALLY CHARGED for any purpose and do not have to be worn to be effective. The main **function** of TALISMANS is to **project** your will onto the *FLEXIBLE FABRIC* of the *UNIVERSE.* The details of PREPARATION and CONSECRATION are less important than the quality of **focus** that you can bring to bear through their **agency**. Rituals using SYMPATHETIC MAGIC help you achieve focus by **attuning** you with the **energies** you wish to work with.

ENTERING THE MAGICAL ARENA

No one can make a powerful talisman without being a MAGE. If you decide to practice this art, you should be aware that **you are entering the deep waters of the magical arena**. To *PADDLE CARELESSLY* in them is to **risk** being *SWEPT AWAY* by powerful and, *for the inexperienced, UNPREDICTABLE CURRENTS.* In order to master magical forces, *it is crucial first to* MASTER ONESELF. The oldest **maxim** of magic is "*Know thyself.*" If we heed this warning, we can PROCEED without FEAR.

Traditional Talismans

TRADITIONALLY, talismans were inscribed on **flat metal** or **stone disks**, but over recent centuries **parchment** has come to be favored in the WEST. There are as many ways to make a talisman as there are different magical traditions in the world, *but in* HERMETIC MAGIC *there are FIVE main types*:

1. ASTROLOGICAL, which are inscribed with the symbols of the **planets** *and/or the signs of the* **zodiac**.

2. MAGICAL, which are inscribed with **sigils** (*magic symbols*), **occult words**, *and/or the names of* **angels**.

3. MIXED, which employ the devices of both the **astrological** and the **magical** talismans.

4. SIGILLA PLANETARUM, which are inscribed with **planetary seals** and **astrological symbols**.

5. HEBREW, which are inscribed with HEBREW **names** and **characters**.

Today, talismans commonly combine most, if not all, of these elements. The talismans described by FRANCIS BARRETT in the highly influential **grimoire**, *The Magus of 1801*, use HEBREW CHARACTERS, PLANETARY SEALS and SYMBOLS, and ANGELIC SIGILS.

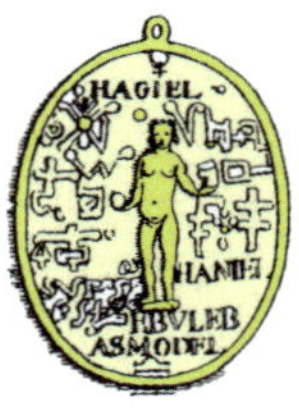

Hebrew Script

HEBREW, like GREEK and RUSSIAN, *is written with its own unique alphabetic script.* The **names** of the planetary angels can be **inscribed** onto a talisman using HEBREW characters (*see pages 162–163*), as well as other magical words. HEBREW *is written from right to left and has few VOWELS.* In HEBREW, the **numbers** one to ten are written with the same symbols as **letters** of the alphabet. For example, **aleph**, the *FIRST LETTER* of the HEBREW alphabet, *is BOTH the letter A and the number 1.* Thus, *NAMES* written in HEBREW also have a **numerical value**. It is this numerical correspondence that is used to create *PLANETARY SEALS* and *ANGELIC SIGILS* (*see overleaf*).

Aleph (A) א	Beth (B) ב	Gimel (G) ג	Daleth (D) ד	Heh (H) ה	Vav (V) ו
Zayin (Z) ז	Cheth (Ch) ח	Teth (T) ט	Yod (Y) י	Kaph (K) כ	Lamed (L) ל
Mem (M) מ	Num (N) נ	Samekh (S) ס	Ayin (O) ע	Peh (P) פ	Tsaddi (Ts) צ
Qoph (Q) ק	Resh (R) ר	Shin (Sh) ש	Tau (T) ת		
Final K ך	Final M ם	Final N ן	Final P ף	Final Ts ץ	

Planetary Seals and Symbols

A magic square, known in KABBALISTIC *magic as a* **kamea**, *is a* GRID *containing different numbers. Each planet has a kamea that* **equals the square of its planetary number**. *For example,* SATURN'S *number is* THREE, *so its kamea is a grid of nine numbers (3 x 3).* **Planetary seals** *are devices that represent the qualities of a particular planet. The seals are designed to* **intersect** *every square on the kamea. Several of the* TRADITIONAL SEALS *have become so stylized that they can no longer do this. Some* MAGES *use the traditional forms of the* SEALS, *while others prefer to* **redraw** *them. The* **planetary symbols** *are those used in astrology.*

example

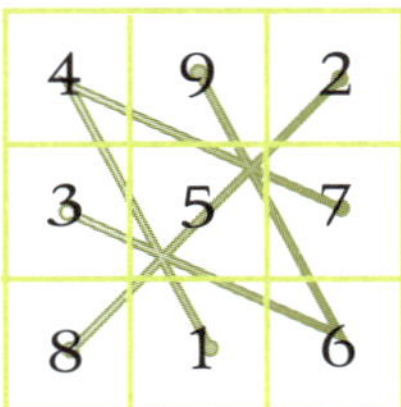

The kamea of Saturn is a grid of nine numbers. Saturn's planetary seal intersects each number on the grid.

saturn

Planetary seal

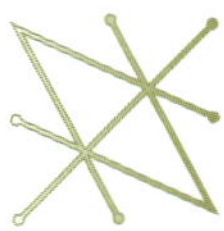

Planetary symbol

♄

Jupiter

Planetary seal

Planetary symbol

♃

Mars

Planetary seal

Planetary symbol

♂

Sun

Planetary seal

Planetary symbol

☉

Venus

Planetary seal

Planetary symbol

♀

Mercury

Planetary seal

Planetary symbol

☿

Moon

Planetary seal

Planetary symbol

☽

Angelic Sigils and Names

Each planet has a host of angels that represents its **energies** and **qualities**. In talismanic magic, *the sigils of the angels that SYMBOLIZE a PLANET'S* **spirit** *and* **intelligence** *are inscribed on the talisman.* The angelic sigils are derived from their PLANETARY KAMEAS by **transcribing** the HEBREW characters of the angelic names numerically, *and* **joining** *up those numbers on the kamea to form the sigil.*

Spirit of Saturn: Zazel

Hebrew name:

זאזל

Intelligence of Jupiter: Yophiel

Hebrew name:

יהפיאל

Intelligence of Saturn: Agiel

Hebrew name:

אגיאל

Spirit of Mars: Bartzabel

Hebrew name:

ברצבאל

Spirit of Jupiter: Hismael

Hebrew name:

הסמאל

Intelligence of Mars: Graphiel

Hebrew name:

גראפיאל

Spirit of the Sun: Sorath

Hebrew name:

סוראת

Intelligence of the Sun: Nakhiel

Hebrew name:

נכיאל

Spirit of Venus: Kedemel

Hebrew name:

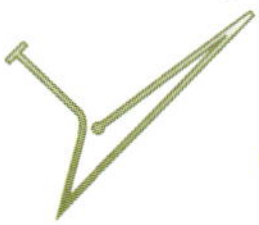

קדמאל

Intelligence of Venus: Hagiel

Hebrew name

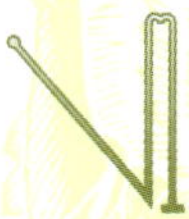

הגיאל

Spirit of Mercury: Taphthartharath

Hebrew name:

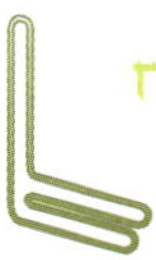

תפתרתרת

Intelligence of Mercury: Tiriel

Hebrew name:

טיריאל

Spirit of the Moon: Chasmodai

Hebrew name:

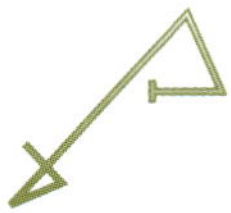

חשמדאי

Intelligence of the Moon: Malkah be-Tarshisim We-ad be-Ruaachoth ha-Schechalim

Hebrew name:

מלכא בתרשיסים ועד ברוחות השחלים

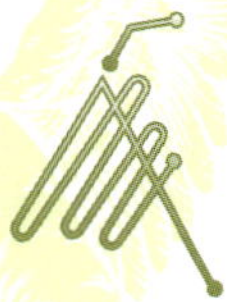

Making a Talisman

Suitable planets for *DEFENSE* against **psychic attack** are VENUS and the SUN. For a more **personal** talisman, you can choose the *RULING PLANET* of your ZODIAC sign (*see page 146*) and adapt the talismans described for VENUS and the SUN *using the correspondences on pages 147–151.*

SOLAR TALISMAN

As the **cosmic** body of LIGHT, CONSCIOUSNESS, and VITALITY, the SUN is ideally suited for protective talismans that *SHIELD you against the dark forces that threaten to undermine your* **health** *and* **well-being**. Traditionally a solar talisman is made from a **disk of pure gold**. Cheaper alternatives are to gild a disk of **walnut** or **ash** wood with *GOLD LEAF*, or to mix fine *GOLD FILINGS* with **clay** or **wax**. All work on the talisman should be **performed** on a SUNDAY, *preferably at dawn. Carefully INSCRIBE on one side of the disk the following*:

1. The planetary seal of the Sun (*see page 161*).
2. The astrological symbol of the Sun (*see page 161*).
3. The angelic sigils of Sorath and Nakhiel (*see page 163*).
4. The Hebrew names of Sorath and Nakhiel (*see page 163*).

On the **reverse** side of the disk inscribe a **hexagram**. This is a protective device known as the SEAL of SOLOMON, because it was ENGRAVED on a **ring** delivered to KING SOLOMON the WISE by the angel RAPHAEL to bind the **demons** plaguing the construction of the **temple**. While you work on the talisman, *keep your mind FOCUSED on its purpose.*

VENUS TALISMAN

The planet of **love** and **affection**, VENUS *is ideally suited to protect you from the ENMITY and HATRED of others.* A VENUS talisman that has been well prepared and consecrated is said to AVERT the danger of **death** *and to be effective in guarding WOMEN against* **cancer**. Traditionally a Venus talisman is made from a **disk of pure copper**. *As copper is INEXPENSIVE and easy to obtain*, do not use a substitute. All work on the talisman should be **performed** on a FRIDAY, *preferably at dawn. Carefully INSCRIBE on one side of the disk the following*:

1. The planetary seal of Venus (*see page 161*).
2. The astrological symbol of Venus (*see page 161*).
3. The angelic sigils of Kedemel and Hagiel (*see page 163*).
4. The Hebrew names of Kedemel and Hagiel (*see page 163*).

On the **reverse** side of the disk, inscribe the seven-pointed star known as the **heptagon**, *which is a symbol of protection that has a SPECIAL AFFINITY with* VENUS.

Consecrating a Talisman

As we have seen with amulets, *talismans need to be PSYCHICALLY CHARGED in order to* **resonate** *with the will of their maker and* **act** *on the INVISIBLE PLANE.* In the case of TALISMANS, this involves a **ritual** of CONSECRATION that can be **performed** in any way you choose. The following traditional ritual is most powerful if preceded by the rituals of ANGELIC INVOCATION described on pages 176–177. *The ritual for a* SOLAR TALISMAN *should be performed at dawn on a* SUNDAY. The ritual for a VENUS TALISMAN should be performed at dawn on a FRIDAY. Again, *use the correspondences on pages 147–151* to *ADAPT* this ritual for other **planetary talismans**.

1. FACING THE EAST, **breathe** seven times on the talisman, saying:
"*By the FIRMAMENT and the spirit of the VOICE,*
be thou unto me as a SIGN of LIGHT and a SEAL of WILL,
affording me protection."

2. TURNING TO THE SOUTH, *expose the talisman to* **incense smoke**. Ideally, the fire should be started by using a **magnifying glass** to focus the RAYS of the DAWN SUN.

SOLAR INCENSE: *CINNAMON, CLOVE, or FRANKINCENSE*, burned over a small fire made from the **twigs** of solar trees, such as **ash** and **laurel**, *and the DRIED stalks of ROSEMARY or any other solar plant (see page 149).*

VENUS INCENSE: *VIOLET or ROSE*, burned on the **twigs** of Venus trees, such as **apple** and **pear**, *and the DRIED stalks of YARROW or any other Venus plant (see page 150).*

3. WHILE HOLDING THE TALISMAN
OVER THE SMOKE, SAY:
"By the BRAZEN SERPENT, before which fell the SERPENTS of FIRE, be thou unto me as a SIGN of LIGHT and a SEAL of WILL, affording me protection."

4. TURNING TO THE WEST, **sprinkle** the talisman with **holy water** (*see pages 186–187*), while saying:
"In the name of ELOHIM [one of the HEBREW names of GOD], and by the spirit of the LIVING WATERS, be thou unto me as a SIGN of LIGHT and a SEAL of WILL, affording me protection."

5. TURNING TO THE NORTH, place a few **grains** of **rock salt** on the talisman and say:
"By the SALT of the EARTH and by virtue of the LIFE ETERNAL, be thou unto me as a SIGN of LIGHT and a SEAL of WILL, affording me protection."

6. AT THE CONCLUSION OF THE RITUAL, place the talisman in a **silk envelope** and either keep it in a *SAFE PLACE or wear it around the NECK attached by a* **silk ribbon**.

SOLAR COLORS: *GOLD or YELLOW SILK ENVELOPE and RIBBON.*
VENUS COLORS: *GREEN or ROSE-COLORED SILK ENVELOPE and RIBBON.*

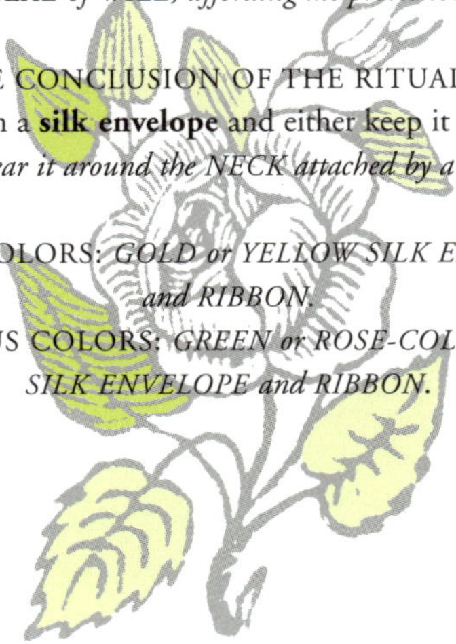

Chapter 7

Angel Magic

The *PLANETARY SPIRITS* and *INTELLIGENCES* discussed in the previous chapter on **talismanic magic** are not the only angels on whom we can call for assistance. *By following the correct* **preparations** *and performing the correct* **rituals**, we can invoke the GREAT ARCHANGELS themselves.

Attunement

Being of great PURITY and INTELLIGENCE, the angelic consciousnesses **vibrate** at extremely high frequencies. *To give yourself the best chance of TUNING into them and* **invoking** *them successfully,* you should prepare yourself through rituals of *PURIFICATION*, such as FASTING, CLEANSING, and PRAYER. Fasting, *as we have seen on pages 126–127,* is very purifying, *but you should take care not to overdo it.* Fasting for a day or two before an INVOCATION is sufficient. *You should do your best to* **avoid** *addictive and stimulating substances for a whole day at least* and keep in mind that certain foods, like ONIONS and GARLIC, **repel all spirits**—*ANGELS no less than VAMPIRES.*

Herbal Preparations

Instead of tea or coffee, *drink herbal infusions,* such as *LEMON BALM, FENNEL, CHAMOMILE,* or *MINT, to calm and tone your system.* You can also add these herbs to purifying, relaxing **baths**. One of the best herbs for this purpose is VERVAIN, a magical substance that RELAXES and TONES the nervous system and *PROMOTES* **clairvoyant dreams**. A scented, CANDLELIT BATH is an ideal preparation for angel magic. *A few drops of OIL of MYRRH diluted in* **water** *taken three times a day is also very* PURIFYING.

Sexual Abstinence

You should also avoid SEXUAL AROUSAL during the purification period. *This is not a MORAL consideration,* simply a question of **vibration**. Humans, like all animals, come in TWOS. To **mate**, we need *ANOTHER HALF.* Angels are ANDROGYNOUS, sexless beings, *complete in themselves.* Sexual **desire** makes us *more* HUMAN and *less* ANGELIC, *which is not CONDUCIVE to angel magic.*

Angelic Script

The angels COMMUNICATE *with us directly, but they are also said to have their own* LANGUAGE*—perhaps more than one, since several have been put forward, including* Enochian, *a* WRITTEN *language* DICTATED *to the* Elizabethan *mages Dee and Kelly by the spirits they were working with. There are several different scripts used for communicating with angels. The* "THEBAN SCRIPT" *is the easiest to use, because its 23* LETTERS *are exactly the same as those of our own* ALPHABET. *The only difference is that it lacks the letters* J, U, *and* W. *For* J, *substitute the Theban character* I; *for* U, *the Theban* V; *and for* W, *write the Theban* V *twice.*

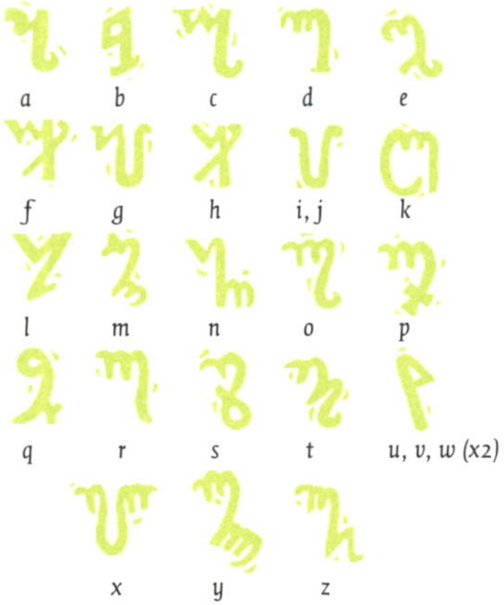

Petitioning an Angel

A **petition** is a written request for help. When addressed to an angel, *a petition will have more resonance*, and therefore be more effective, *if it is written in angelic script*. The first thing to do is **decide** which ANGEL you wish to petition. For example, *if you wish to be PROTECTED against EVIL*, you can petition LAHABIEL, the angel of protection. Other helpful angels include:

ARIEL *Angel of healing*
ARMISAEL *Angel of childbirth*
MIHR *Angel of friendship*
RAHMIEL *Angel of compassion*
SABRAEL *Angel of healing*
SERAPHIEL *Angel of peace*
TAHARIEL *Angel of purity*
VASIARIAH *Angel of mercy*
YEHUDIAH *Angel of bereavement*
ZARUCH *Angel of strength*

This simple blueprint can be applied to any situation:
In the name of.........[GOD/ALLAH/JESUS CHRIST/ CREATOR/GODDESS, or any other divine name],
I humbly petition you, great angel [insert name]
To [state wish].
I honor you and thank you for receiving my prayer,
In the name of [divine name of choice].

Date your petition and **sign** it. *Petitions should be written on PLAIN pieces of PAPER.* Put your petition in an **envelope** together with any RELEVANT or CORRESPONDING ITEMS that you feel may help your petition.

The Pentagram Ritual

The five-pointed star or pentagram is an ANCIENT SYMBOL *of protection and good luck. It represents the* FIVE SENSES, MAN *as* MICROCOSM, *and the* IMAGE *of* GOD. *It is used in a ritual to form a protective circle of power, much like the* MEDICINE WHEEL *in Native American tradition. It focuses and contains creative spiritual energy prior to performing an invocation. By invoking the* FOUR GREAT ARCHANGELS *with four of the holy* HEBREW NAMES *of* GOD, *it establishes a connection with the elemental forces of nature, while cleansing the aura of all lower elemental interference and infusing one with divine light. The ritual is traditionally begun by performing the* CROSS *of* LIGHT.

The Cross of Light

The Cross of Light is a very effective KABBALISTIC EXERCISE *for strengthening the* **aura** *and focusing* **energy**. It is traditionally performed *PRIOR* to all ritual work, particularly the tracing of a MAGIC CIRCLE.

1. STAND facing EAST and *IMAGINE* a brilliant white light above you. RAISE your **right hand** above your **head** and draw the light down to your **forehead**, saying:

   "Thine, O Lord…"

2. FEEL the light FILL your **head** and *DRAW* it down in a *LINE* through your **body** toward your **feet**, saying:

   "Is the Kingdom…"

3. FEEL the light FILL your **body** and *FOLLOW* your **hand** as you bring it up to your **right shoulder**, saying:

   "The Power…"

4. DRAW the line of LIGHT straight across to your **left shoulder**, saying:

   "And the Glory…"

5. Now CUP your HANDS to your **heart**, feeling the great cross of light *RADIATING* through you, and say:

   "Forever. Amen."

Tracing a Magic Circle

After performing the CROSS of LIGHT, stand facing *EAST* and perform the main part of the pentagram ritual to form a *MAGIC CIRCLE.*

1. Point with either hand, **arm outstretched**, *to a point slightly higher than your head.* Now trace a **pentagram**, IN A CONTINUOUS LINE, starting at the bottom left corner and imagining it as a *LINE* of *FIRE.*

2. Pointing at the CENTER of the BLAZING PENTAGRAM, say in a loud, confident voice:

"*In the name of the Almighty*
YEH-HOH-WAH
And Archangel RAPHAEL, Prince of Air
I draw this circle in the East."

3. Keeping your **arm raised**, turn to the SOUTH, tracing a QUARTER CIRCLE of FLAME. *Now trace another pentagram in the same way.* Again, point to the center of the pentagram, saying:

"*In the name of the Almighty*
AH-DON-EYE
And Archangel MICHAEL, Prince of Fire
I draw this circle in the South."

4. With your arm **still raised**, turn to the WEST, tracing another QUARTER CIRCLE of FLAME. Trace the **pentagram** and pointing at its center say:

> *"In the name of the Almighty*
> *EH-EE-YAY*
> *And Archangel GABRIEL, Prince of Water*
> *I draw this circle in the West."*

5. Keeping your arm raised, turn to the NORTH, tracing another QUARTER CIRCLE of FLAME. Trace the **pentagram** and pointing at its center say:

> *"In the name of the Almighty*
> *AH-GOO-LA*
> *And Archangel URIEL, Prince of Earth*
> *I draw this circle in the North."*

Invoking the Archangels

Once you have drawn a MAGIC CIRCLE, you should **invoke** the ARCHANGELS to create a powerfully **sacred space**.

1. Keeping your arm raised, **turn** once more to the EAST, completing the CIRCLE of FLAME, which now surrounds you with **fiery stars** at each CARDINAL POINT. Now open your arms wide and say:

"Before me RAPHAEL"
[visualize a brilliant yellow light with a violet aura]

"Behind me GABRIEL"
[visualize a brilliant blue light with an orange aura]

"On my right MICHAEL"
[visualize a brilliant red light with a green aura]

"On my left Uriel"
[visualize a brilliant green light with a reddish brown aura]

"Above me the FATHER"
[visualize a fiery hexagram—a six-pointed star composed of two interlocking triangles]

"Below me the MOTHER"
[again visualize a fiery hexagram]

"Within me the Eternal Flame."

2. You have now created a *SACRED SPACE* from which you can **safely invoke** the ANGEL of your choice.

INVOKING LAHABIEL

Any ANGEL may be invoked within the sacred circle. There is no set formula for invocation. The most important thing is that your **words** should **resonate** with PURPOSE and SINCERITY. Below is an example of how to invoke the angel LAHABIEL, *who is traditionally invoked to WARD OFF EVIL SPIRITS.* An angel of the First Day, *SUNDAY*, working under ARCHANGEL MICHAEL, LAHABIEL has specific duties as a "**jinxbuster**" and can be a *POWERFUL ALLY.* The best time to invoke his assistance is on *SUNDAY*, **ideally at dawn**.

"In the name of the ONE,
The ALMIGHTY CREATOR of all,
I invoke you great angel LAHABIEL,
As the angel of protection,
To watch over me and
Deliver me from all evil,
That I might walk the Path of Love
Unthreatened and unharmed.
For this I thank you with all my heart,
In the name of the ALMIGHTY."

When the invocation is complete, CLOSE the RITUAL by performing the CROSS of LIGHT once more (*see page 173*).

Chapter 8
EXORCISM

Exorcism involves the **expulsion** of unwelcome **negative entities**, such as GHOSTS, DEMONS, and DISEASE SPIRITS, from people, animals, objects, or places. **Religions** and **cultures** all over the world have practiced it since the earliest times. *The world's two most ancient civilizations,* EGYPT *and* BABYLON, were the first masters of the art of exorcism.

How Exorcism Works

Exorcism involves **prayers** and **adjurations** (*commands*) recited in the name of the highest divine authority and its intermediaries, *in order to COMPEL a POSSESSING SPIRIT to* **relinquish** *its hold over its victim.* In ancient EGYPT, magical practitioners called upon the mages IMHOTEP and KHONSU for aid in exorcisms.

Spirits are able to possess a person so completely that they can SPEAK through their voices and CONTROL their physical actions. *Exorcising such POWERFUL ENTITIES is no easy matter.* An EXPERIENCED EXORCIST with a profound knowledge of *DEMONOLOGY* may be able to recognize a possessing demon by its VOICE, MODE of SPEECH, SMELL, and SUPERNATURAL POWERS. If the exorcist is able to **name the demon** or force it to name itself, *he or she has a much better chance of achieving success.*

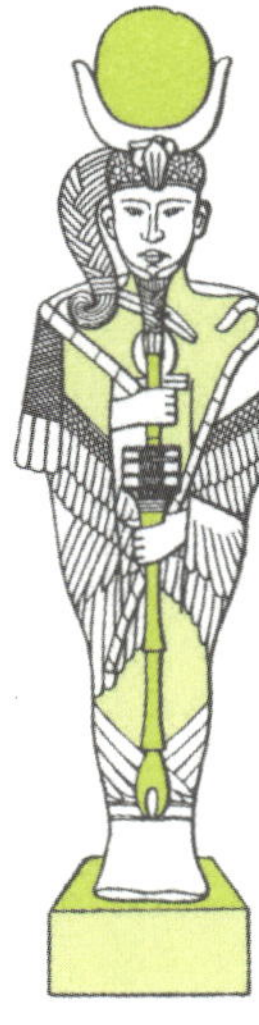

Exorcism and Christianity

The NEW TESTAMENT teaches that JESUS was an exorcist who began his mission by preaching and "*casting out devils.*" The first of Christ's many recorded **miracles** in the GOSPELS took place in the **synagogue at Capernaum** *and engendered his initial fame.* Those who witnessed the event were amazed and asked:

"What new doctrine is this? For with authority commandeth he even the unclean spirits, and they do obey him." And immediately his fame spread abroad throughout all the region round about Galilee. Mark, 1:27–28

JESUS clearly shared his people's belief in disease spirits when he "*rebuked*" the fever of SIMON PETER'S mother-in-law and **healed** her (*Luke 4:39*). He gave his disciples authority to **perform exorcisms** and declared of his believers: "*In my name shall they CAST OUT devils*" (*Mark, 16:17*).

It was natural then that exorcism should be INCORPORATED into early CHRISTIAN DOCTRINE. The ROMAN CATHOLIC ordination of exorcists concludes with the words: "*Take now the power of LAYING HANDS upon the energumens* [possessed people], *and by the imposition of your hands, by the grace of the HOLY SPIRIT, and the words of exorcism, the unclean spirits are driven from OBSESSED bodies.*"

Exorcism Today

Today, many CHRISTIAN PRIESTS and MINISTERS are trained in the techniques of exorcism. *In Britain in 1963, the* ANGLICAN BISHOP of EXETER *convened a commission to consider the theology and techniques of exorcism.* **The commission's findings**, published in 1972, concluded that every bishop should appoint a priest as DIOCESAN EXORCIST and provide him with *SUITABLE TRAINING*. Exorcisms were not to be performed without the **prior consent** of the bishop and only after the possibility of MENTAL or PHYSICAL ILLNESS had been excluded. This latter consideration reflects the position of more *RATIONALISTIC ANGLICANS, many of whom share the view of* **mainstream psychology** *that possession is a symptom of mental problems such as* **multiple personality disorder**.

EVANGELICAL CHRISTIANITY, particularly PENTECOSTALISM, is less cautious in its beliefs and does not observe the same degree of official control exercised by the Roman Catholic, Anglican, and mainstream Protestant churches. *Ministers, or even lay persons, can become exorcists.* In CHARISMATIC CHURCHES, exorcism has become **institutionalized** as a form of "*spiritual warfare.*"

Roman Catholic Exorcism

There are as many different forms of EXORCISM as there are different CREEDS. *The most famous is, perhaps, the Roman Catholic ritual that is outlined here in ABRIDGED FORM.* **Note** that the key aspects are the invocation of divine authority, the **rebuking** and **adjuration** of the possessing entity, and the **praying** on behalf of the possessed. *The full text of the traditional Roman Catholic exorcism ritual can be found on the Internet by searching these keywords*: **Roman ritual exorcism**. Alternately, inquire at your local public library.

INVOCATION

1. **The exorcising priest** is first required to PERFORM CONFESSION and PRAY. Dressed in *SURPLICE* and *PURPLE STOLE*, he traces the sign of the cross over the **energumen** (*the possessed person, who is bound if dangerous*), himself, and the bystanders, *and then sprinkles all present with holy water.*

2. **The priest kneels** and recites the *LITANY* of the *SAINTS*, asking for their intercession, *followed by a prayer for* **deliverance**.

3. **He recites Psalm 53**.

4. **The priest says**: "*GOD, whose nature is ever merciful and forgiving, accept our prayer that this servant of yours, bound by the fetters of sin, may be pardoned by your loving kindness*" and **prays** that GOD "*strike terror into the beast.*"

Rebuke

1. The priest then commands the demon, saying:
"*I command you, unclean spirit, whoever you are, along with all your minions now attacking this servant of GOD, by the mysteries of the incarnation, passion, resurrection, and ascension of our LORD JESUS CHRIST by the descent of the HOLY SPIRIT, by the coming of our LORD for judgment, that you tell me by some sign your name, and the day and hour of your departure. I command you, moreover, to obey me to the letter, I who am a minister of GOD despite my unworthiness; nor shall you be emboldened to harm in any way this creature of GOD, or the bystanders, or any of their possessions.*"

2. The priest lays his hand on the head of the sick person, saying: "*They shall lay their hands upon the sick and all will be well with them. May JESUS, SON of* MARY, *LORD and SAVIOR of the world, through the merits and intercession of His holy apostles PETER and PAUL and all His SAINTS, show you favor and mercy.*"

3. Next he reads selections from the Gospels to the energumen.

4. He then blesses the energumen and sprinkles him or her with holy water.

5. Crossing himself and the energumen, the priest places the end of his stole on the latter's neck, and, *putting his right hand on his head*, he says in a voice filled with CONFIDENCE and FAITH: "*See the CROSS of the LORD; begone, you hostile powers!*"

ADJURATION

1. The priest then performs the following exorcising adjuration (+ *indicates making the sign of the cross with the index and middle fingers*):

"*I cast you out, unclean spirit, along with every satanic power of the enemy, every specter from hell, and all your fell companions; in the name of our LORD + JESUS CHRIST. Begone and stay far from this creature of GOD. + For it is* HE *who commands you,* HE *who flung you headlong from the heights of heaven into the depths of hell. It is* HE *who commands you,* HE *who once stilled the sea and the wind and the storm. Harken, therefore, and tremble in fear, SATAN, you enemy of the faith, you foe of the human race, you begetter of death, you robber of life, you corrupter of justice, you root of all evil and vice; seducer of men, betrayer of nations, instigator of envy, font of avarice, fomenter of discord, author of pain and sorrow. Why, then, do you stand and resist, knowing as you must that CHRIST the LORD brings your plans to nothing? Fear* HIM, *who in ISAAC was offered in sacrifice, in JOSEPH sold into bondage, slain as the paschal lamb, crucified as man, yet triumphed over the powers of hell.* [The following three signs of the cross are traced on the brow of the energumen.] *Begone, then, in the name of the FATHER, + and of the SON, + and of the HOLY + SPIRIT. Give place to the HOLY SPIRIT by this sign of the holy + cross of our LORD JESUS CHRIST, who lives and reigns with the FATHER and the HOLY SPIRIT, GOD, forever and ever.* AMEN."

2. **Further prayers and adjurations follow**, during which the DEVIL is ADDRESSED variously as: "*ancient serpent, transgressor, seducer, foe of virtue, persecutor of the innocent, abominable creature, monster,*" and so on.

3. **These lengthy adjurations are repeated as often as necessary**, until the ENERGUMEN has been *FULLY FREED*.

4. **While various prayers are recited**, the priest SPRINKLES the home of the energumen with HOLY WATER and *BURNS INCENSE*.

Conclusion

1. **Following the energumen's deliverance**, the priest prays: "*Almighty GOD, we beg you to keep the evil spirit from further molesting this servant of yours, and to keep him far away, never to return. At your command, O LORD, may the goodness and peace of our LORD JESUS CHRIST, our REDEEMER, take possession of this man/woman. May we no longer fear any evil since the LORD is with us; who lives and reigns with you, in the unity of the HOLY SPIRIT, GOD, forever and ever.*"

2. **Everyone present at the exorcism says** "AMEN."

Holy Water

Holy water, also called **lustral water**, is used during exorcisms. *You can use it to protect your home and yourself from negative spirits.* The RITUAL for PREPARING holy water is performed in many faiths and traditions. *Common to most of these traditions is the addition of CONSECRATED SALT.* In the JUDEO-CHRISTIAN tradition, this practice can be traced back to the biblical account in II Kings, 2:19–21, **where the prophet** ELISHA **used salt to purify the unclean water of a well**.

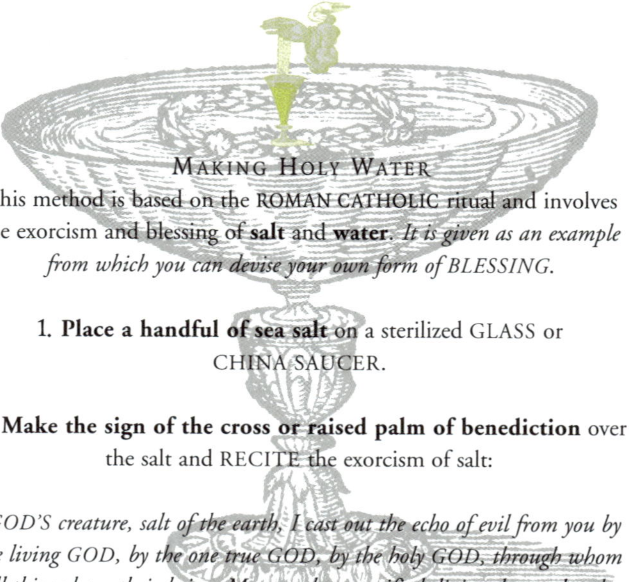

Making Holy Water

This method is based on the ROMAN CATHOLIC ritual and involves the exorcism and blessing of **salt** and **water**. *It is given as an example from which you can devise your own form of BLESSING.*

1. **Place a handful of sea salt** on a sterilized GLASS or CHINA SAUCER.

2. **Make the sign of the cross or raised palm of benediction** over the salt and RECITE the exorcism of salt:

"GOD'S creature, salt of the earth, I cast out the echo of evil from you by the living GOD, by the one true GOD, by the holy GOD, through whom all things have their being. May you be a purified, living, heavenly salt, a means of health for those who believe, a medicine for body and soul for all who make use of you. May all evil fancies be driven far from the place where you are sprinkled. And let every unclean spirit be repulsed by the power of ALMIGHTY GOD."

3. Recite the blessing of salt:

"*Almighty everlasting GOD, I humbly appeal to your mercy and goodness to bless this creature, salt, that you have given for humankind's use. May all who use it find in it a remedy for body and mind. And may everything that it touches be freed from uncleanness and any influence of evil through your holy name.* AMEN."

4. Make the sign of the cross or raised palm of benediction over a sterilized GLASS BOWL of fresh spring water and repeat the exorcism of salt (*step 2*), EXCHANGING *the word salt for water.*

5. Recite the blessing of water:

"*O GOD, who for man's welfare established the most wonderful mysteries in the substance of water, hearken to this prayer, and pour forth your blessing on this element. May this creature of yours, when used in your mysteries and endowed with your grace, serve to cast out demons and to banish disease. May everything that this water touches be delivered from all that is unclean and hurtful; through your holy name.* AMEN."

6. Now pour the salt into the water in the form of a cross, saying:

"*May this heavenly salt and water unite in harmony, in the name of the ALMIGHTY GOD.* AMEN."

Index

BIBLIOGRAPHY

African Religions and Philosophy, John S. Mbiti

The Book of Angels, Francis Melville

The Book of Vodou, Leah Gordon

Cagliostro, W.R.H. Trowbridge

A Dictionary of Angels, Gustav Davidson

Divine Horsemen: The Living Gods of Haiti, Maya Deren

Encyclopedia of Occultism and Parapsychology, J. Gordon Melton

The Encyclopedia of Religion, Mircea Eliade (ed.)

Frabato the Magician, Franz Bardon

The Golden Bough: A study in Magic and Religion, Sir James G. Frazer

The Golden Builders, Tobias Churton

Initiation into Hermetics, Franz Bardon

Introduction to Magic: Rituals and Practical Techniques for the Magus, Julius Evola et al

Liber 777, Aleister Crowley

The Magus, Francis Barrett

The Malleus Maleficarum, Montague Summers (ed.)

On the Mysteries, Iamblichus (translated by Thomas Taylor)

The Origins of Freemasonry, David Stevenson

The Philosophy of Natural Magic, Henry Cornelius Agrippa

Picatrix (Ghâyat al-Hakîm Fi'l-sihr or Aim of the Wise), Maslamah ibn Ahmad Majriti

The Practical Handbook of Plant Alchemy, Manfred M. Junius

Psychic Self-Defense, Dion Fortune

Real Magic, P.E.I. Bonewitz

The Rosicrucian Enlightenment, Frances A. Yates

The Satanic Bible, Anton LaVey

Satanic Panic: The Creation of a Contemporary Legend, Jeffrey Victor

The Secret Lore of Magic, Idries Shah

The Secrets of High Magic, Francis Melville

Speak of the Devil: Tales of Satanic Abuse in Contemporary England, Jean la Fontaine

The Triumph of the Moon: A History of Modern Pagan Witchcraft, Ronald Hutton

Vampires, Burial, and Death: Folklore and Reality, Paul Barber

Witchcraft and Magic in Europe: The 20th Century, Willem de Blecourt et al

Witchcraft, Magic, and Alchemy, Grillot de Givry

Witches, Devils, and Doctors in the Renaissance (De Praestigiis Daemonum), Johann Weyer